LARGE PRINT

LS

SHOOT-OUT

Mike Faraday, the laconic L.A. private investigator, becomes involved in mayhem and murder after taxidermist Abel Cramp finds a small fortune in jewellery concealed in the crop of a rare mountain eagle, sent to him for mounting. Mike's search for the answers leads to a millionaire's estate in the hills. On the way, he meets a corpse in a cupboard and a huge woman who can kill men with one blow of her massive fist, not to mention two professional hitmen who try to incinerate him at the bottom of a canyon.

BASIL COPPER

SHOOT-OUT

Complete and Unabridged

LINFORD
Leicester

First published in Great Britain in 1982

First Linford Edition
published 2005

British Library CIP Data

Copper, Basil
  Shoot-out.—Large print ed.—
  Linford mystery library
  1. Faraday, Mike (Fictitious character)—Fiction
  2. Private investigators—California—Los Angeles
  —Fiction 3. Detective and mystery stories
  4. Large type books
  I. Title
  823.9′14 [F]

  ISBN 1–84395–756–6

Published by
F. A. Thorpe (Publishing)
Anstey, Leicestershire

Set by Words & Graphics Ltd.
Anstey, Leicestershire
Printed and bound in Great Britain by
T. J. International Ltd., Padstow, Cornwall

This book is printed on acid-free paper

1

'There's a character called Abel Cramp on the line,' Stella said.

'That's his misfortune,' I told her.

Stella smiled, holding her hand over the receiver of the phone on her desk.

'So we got enough work now not to bother about any more cases,' she told the filing cabinet.

I stirred myself in my swivel chair behind my old broadtop and took my gaze off the cracks in the ceiling.

'Maybe you're right, honey,' I said. 'What does he want?'

'That's the trouble,' Stella said. 'He won't say. He wants to speak to you personally.'

I picked up my own instrument, listening to the heavy breathing at the other end.

'Faraday here,' I said.

'At last,' a rusty-sounding voice said. 'You're a hard man to reach, Mr Faraday.'

'These are hard times,' I said. 'What's your problem?'

1

'Not so fast,' the voice went on. 'We haven't talked about rates yet.'

'We haven't talked about your case yet,' I said.

Stella tossed the gold bell of her hair and put her phone down. She went over to the glassed-in alcove where we do the brewing-up, her heels beating a stirring tattoo on the floor. I admired her action all the way.

'You have a point, Mr Faraday,' the rusty voice went on. 'I run a small business over on the edge of town. I'm not a rich man.'

'Who is these days?' I said. 'I'd still like to know your problem.'

'It's not something I can talk about over the phone,' the voice went on.

'I'm getting a little tired of this conversation,' I said. 'What would you suggest? I hear the phone rates are going up in the fall.'

'There's no call for that attitude, Mr Faraday,' the voice continued waspishly. 'It's just that I'm in something of a quandary.'

'Tell you what,' I said. 'It's a beautiful

morning. Take an hour off from whatever you're doing and drag your underwear over here and I'll listen to your troubles.'

Cramp chuckled hoarsely.

'A great sense of humour, Mr Faraday.'

'I try,' I told him. 'Can you make it?'

'I can make it,' Cramp said. 'And it won't cost me anything?'

I stared at Stella. She was back from the alcove now and sat on the edge of her own desk listening incredulously to the conversation.

'It won't cost you anything to talk to me,' I said. 'I can promise you that much.'

I glanced over to where the brilliant sun stencilled the pattern of the blinds on the floor. The plastic-bladed fan pecked tiredly at the edges of the silence and the muted hum of stalled traffic came up from the boulevard below. It was a typical day with a typical atmosphere; one third smog; one third gasoline fumes; and one third California climate.

'Excellent, Mr Faraday,' Cramp said. 'After lunch. You can expect me around three o'clock if that will be convenient.'

'That's fine,' I said. 'I'll be waiting.'

I put the phone down before he could go on. Stella sat staring at me for a few seconds longer, her eyes very bright.

'So we got one of those, Mike,' she said. 'There won't be much gravy on this one.'

'It's been a tough quarter,' I said. 'I'm not choosy.'

Stella smiled and went back over to the alcove. I waited, salivating slightly as I smelt the aroma of fresh-roasted coffee beans. It's my favourite moment of the day and today was no exception.

She came back after a while and put my coffee down on the blotter, pushed over the biscuit tin. I rooted around for one of my favourites. Stella got her own cup, sat down in the client's chair the other side of my desk and stirred the sugar in thoughtfully.

I put a butternut fudge in my mouth and took a tentative bite. It was up to the usual standard. Little traces of the smile remained around the corners of Stella's mouth at my expression. I could have watched it all day but I had other things on my plate. I put my cup down with a faint chinking noise.

'Isn't Cramp something to do with the taxidermy business?' Stella said.

I looked at her in surprise.

'I didn't know he was famous.'

Stella shook her head.

'He isn't, goof,' she said. 'It's just that I was looking something up in the phonebook yesterday. Under C, of course. His name must have been in an adjacent column because it rings a bell.'

She got up and collected the volume from her own desk. I sat and stared at the decor while she riffled the pages. Like I'd said it had been a rough quarter and apart from a few outstanding debts Faraday Investigations hadn't a thing on its books. Except dust, of course. We always have problems with the cleaning. I shifted the seat of my pants in my swivel chair and focused up on Stella. It's always a pleasure and today was no exception.

'I thought I was right,' she said. 'Apparently he runs a high-class taxidermy operation. He has an office number and a workshop number.'

She made a note on her pad.

'Has he,' I said. 'Then why was he crabbing about money?'

Stella smiled again.

'That's how he runs a high-class business. By worrying about the dollars.'

'I'd like to see one,' I said. 'I'm running on cents at the moment.'

Stella shook her head.

'It's not that bad, Mike. Don't exaggerate. You haven't touched the deposit account yet.'

'That's for emergencies,' I said.

Stella stared thoughtfully at her note-pad.

'Maybe this is an emergency,' she said.

'We shall see,' I told her.

   ★ ★ ★

Abel Cramp, when I got to see him, was an extraordinary sight. He arrived soon after three and when Stella showed him in from the waiting-room, he stood blinking waterily and looking warily from me to Stella and back again.

'Mr Faraday?'

'That's what it says on the door,' I told him.

He grinned, showing very yellow teeth, like I'd made a joke. He was a tall, thin, loose-made man who looked like a puppet which had been badly wired up. I waved him into the client's chair and he undulated awkwardly forward, like he might collapse at any moment.

He had a narrow, lined face which made him resemble a puppet more than ever and his dusty-white hair appeared to have been pasted down to his skull. He was dressed in a loose-fitting salt and pepper suit that emphasised the dusty, dried-up effect and he had an annoying habit of clicking his teeth every half minute or so. I could have done without Abel Cramp this afternoon but I was lumbered with him and had to make the best of it.

'All right, Mr Cramp,' I said, when he had settled himself. 'What can I do for you?'

He mopped his forehead with a none too clean handkerchief.

'I don't really know yet, Mr Faraday,'

he said, looking worriedly at Stella.

'Does she have to be here?'

I grinned.

'She works here.'

He shook his head again. Stella was having a job to keep a straight face. She wore a pale blue dress today and the material went in and out in all the right places. She looked as cool and fresh as a spring morning in the High Sierras. You're getting in your Emily Dickinson mood again, Mike, I told myself.

'You didn't answer my question, Mr Faraday.'

'The answer's yes,' I told him. 'She stays here. She's part of my organisation.'

I paused, choosing my words carefully.

'You might almost say she is my organisation.'

Stella turned a faint pink beneath her tan and went to sit down at her own desk. She looked at me thoughtfully as she cupped her chin on her hands.

Abel Cramp blew his cheeks in and out a few times like he was having difficulty with his words.

'Very well, Mr Faraday. But I'm not

used to having pretty girls around me.'

'You should try it,' I told him. 'It's extremely pleasant.'

He glared at me from under his thatch of grey steelwool for a moment like he was mortally offended. But I guess he was hard to offend because he took another tack almost straight away.

'Let's get to business, Mr Faraday. I run a taxidermy setup. Pretty high-class work, which runs to museums and institutions as well as private individuals.'

'I know,' I said. 'We already looked you up.'

Cramp stopped in mid-stride and stared at me with what seemed like alarm in his eyes.

'You know me, Mr Faraday?'

I shook my head.

'Nothing like that. It's just that we like to get the background of people with whom we're dealing. The young lady checked you out from yellow pages.'

He made the ugly clicking noise with his teeth.

'Ah! I see.'

He frowned at me suspiciously.

'When I described my work, I didn't mean to imply that I'm a wealthy man. I'll pay you a fair price but I'm not rich.'

'I have a standard rate,' I said. 'Let's get to the meat.'

Cramp drew his feet in with an agitated movement. For a minute I thought he was going to fall off his hooks but he recovered himself.

'Now I don't know whether you know anything about taxidermy, Mr Faraday. It's almost a passion with me.'

'Spare me the eulogies,' I said. 'Let's take it you just like stuffing things.'

The old boy glared at me and Stella went into a sudden fit of coughing. Cramp recovered himself first.

'Somewhat crudely put, Mr Faraday,' he said stiffly. 'We're getting off the point. This is about some specimens which have just arrived. They were refrigerated, of course, and we started work on them this morning.'

'What were they?' I said.

Abel Cramp stiffened.

'I was coming to that.'

He paused and glanced over his

10

shoulder like Stella shouldn't have been listening. I noticed she'd started taking notes.

'Before I confide in you, Mr Faraday, there is a little problem.'

He moistened his lips with a blue tongue.

'About the specimens?' I said.

He nodded.

'Not to put too fine a point on it, they were birds. Extremely large birds.'

I sat back in my swivel chair and held his eyes with my own.

'You don't have to spell it out to me, Mr Cramp. They were eagles, weren't they? Of a rare type.'

He nodded again, without speaking.

'In other words, protected birds,' I said. 'You needn't worry, Mr Cramp. I don't like what you've told me but I'm not a moralist and I'm not the official law. I presume you want to tell me something other than that?'

Cramp held out one stringy hand in a placatory gesture.

'I thought it best to make the situation quite clear, Mr Faraday. I won't specify what the birds were. Suffice it to say that they were large ones, or I should not be here on my present errand. Where was I?'

'They'd been sent you for mounting up,' I said.

'Oh, yes. Well, the customer was a big client of mine, who sends me a great deal of work during the course of the year. And he pays well; very well indeed.'

'I thought you weren't a rich man?' I said.

Cramp winced as though I'd struck him. Stella's smile hovered on her lips for almost half a minute.

'I have a large staff to maintain,' Cramp said evenly, his eyes fixed up on the ceiling.

'The point I'm making, Mr Faraday, is that I could not afford to ignore my client's wishes. Their Director, Mr Vansittart, had already phoned the day before.'

'Who is your client?' I said.

'I'll get to that later,' Cramp said.

He drew his chair nearer to the edge of my desk.

'Now, I want you to understand precisely my dilemma, Mr Faraday. I do get such work from time to time. I have to turn a blind eye, as it were. And my staff also. Which is expensive.'

'You have to pay them to keep their mouths shut,' I said.

Cramp winced again and looked half-back across his shoulder at Stella.

'This sort of work is carried out by my head mounter, Couzens, and myself in person,' he said. 'We work in an inner room on such commissions so that the rest of the staff don't know. I want you to be quite clear about this.'

'There is a point to it all?' I said.

Cramp looked pained.

'Most certainly, Mr Faraday. I'm just trying to localise the circumstances for you. That leaves the staff in Mr Vansittart's premises, who would be very few you understand; the people who deliver the specimens; and myself and Couzens. These were the only people who had contact with the specimens. I can leave out the delivery people, of course, because the refrigerated container was locked.'

I drummed with my fingers on my

blotter and stared at the sun-dazzle on the blinds behind Cramp's head, resisting the urge to throw something at him. Still, I had nothing else to do this afternoon and it was as good a way of passing the time as any.

'All right,' I said. 'These two rare, illegal eagles arrived and you set to work on them. What then?'

Cramp opened his mouth angrily, then shut it with a snap, making a remorseless thin line of his lips. It didn't make him look any more attractive.

'I won't go into all the procedures we go through in preparing specimens, Mr Faraday.'

'That's something to be grateful for,' I said. 'I had a particularly rich lunch.'

Cramp glared again but he plunged on doggedly.

'My assistant prepared the smaller of the two birds; I began work on the second. When he'd finished the preparatory work on his specimen he was called away to the telephone. It was then I found something peculiar in the crop of my bird. Three things to be precise.'

'Such as what?' I said.

Cramp smiled thinly.

'Such as these, Mr Faraday.'

He produced a grubby handkerchief from his pocket and opened it. A rain of white and silver fire cascaded on to my blotter. I heard Stella give a little gasp. I sat staring at the three-row diamond necklace and matching diamond earrings until my eyes were dazzled.

2

There was a silence in the office so heavy it seemed like a storm was about to break. Stella got up from her desk and came over to mine. She picked up the necklace with slightly trembling fingers.

'That must be worth a fortune,' I said.

'It is, Mike,' Stella said in a low voice. 'These are genuine all right. There's no doubt about it.'

Cramp smirked, pleased at the effect he'd created.

'The young lady should know, Mr Faraday. Now, what do you think of that?'

'I can't come up with anything plausible at the moment,' I said. 'But I'm working on it.'

Stella was holding the necklace to the light. Her eyes were dreamy as she glanced down at me.

'They should be worth around 100,000 dollars, Mike.'

Abel Cramp looked like he was going

to have a seizure. He clicked his teeth two or three times and something like a palsy agitated his frame.

'Well, well, Mr Faraday.'

'We'd better hang on to these, Mr Cramp,' I said. 'We'll give you an official receipt for them, of course.'

Cramp looked at me suspiciously.

'I don't know about that, Mr Faraday.'

I grinned.

'You brought the stuff in. Which proves you're an honest man. Don't give me reason to doubt it.'

Cramp looked at me indignantly.

'Since we're being offensive,' he snapped. 'How do I know what you're going to do with those gems?'

I shook my head.

'You don't, Mr Cramp. But just use a little common sense. They're going in my safe and then into the bank. They'll stay there until we hand them over to the police. They're bound to be stolen property.'

Cramp stared from me to Stella. He looked like the idea was incredible to him.

17

'I don't understand.'

'You're not suggesting that eagle could have swallowed all that stuff in the natural course of events,' I said, looking at the string of pale fire suspended from Stella's fingers.

Cramp shook his head, his teeth clamped tightly together. He was on firm ground now.

'Of course not, Mr Faraday. Quite impossible. Eagles are big birds but this one couldn't have swallowed these items without choking.'

'How do you think they got there?' I said.

Cramp swivelled in the chair, his eyes still fixed on the diamond necklace.

'The bird hadn't been cut in any way. It could have been done by forcing the jewellery down with a rod or similar instrument. It would have had to have been done very carefully.'

I fixed my gaze on to the cracks in the ceiling.

'That rules out absolutely any accidental means by which that stuff could have got there,' I said.

'We could check the stolen property lists,' Stella said. 'I'll make a start on that just as soon as Mr Cramp has left.'

Cramp fixed her with a gimlet eye.

'I shan't do that until I've got my receipt,' he snapped.

'We would never dream of letting you go without it,' said Stella imperturbably.

She went over to her own desk, got out the official receipt book, the special one we use to impress the clients and started scribbling in it. Cramp sat defensively hunched up in the client's chair, looking from me to Stella uneasily. His grey, pasted-down hair and salt and pepper suit made him look as anonymous as a pebble on a beach.

'This is a matter of extreme discretion, Mr Faraday,' he said after a moment or two. 'I don't quite know how to handle this.'

'That's why you came to me,' I reminded him. 'So where are we at? This character Vansittart, whose address you're going to give me, sent you two rare mountain eagles for preservation. The birds were protected, which makes the set-up illegal, but we'll overlook that. In one of the specimens you found about a hundred thousand bucks' worth of diamond jewellery, probably stolen.'

Stella came back over, gave Cramp his receipt. She picked up the set of earrings with a wistful expression on her face.

'Total value approximately 150,000 dollars, Mike,' she said in the same dreamy voice as before. 'I've put the estimated value down on the receipt.'

Cramp glanced at it sharply, folded it and put it in a shabby pigskin wallet he took out an inner pocket.

'I presume these jewels are fully insured while they're in your care, Mr Faraday?'

'Sure,' I said. 'We'll all be covered. You'll see the policy details set out clearly if you look at the receipt.'

Cramp cleared his throat nervously, little spots of red starting out on his cheekbones. He looked like one of the puppet characters from Petrouchka for a moment.

'Quite so, Mr Faraday. Now, where have we got to?'

'Not very far,' I said. 'You were going to give me Vansittart's address.'

Cramp drummed with pale, quivering fingers on the surface of my desk. Stella picked up the items of jewellery and put them in a big manila envelope. Cramp said nothing but his eyes followed her all the way across the room while she locked them in the safe. She came back and gave me a faint smile.

'They'll be going in the bank first thing in the morning,' she told the filing cabinet.

I was getting a little tired of Cramp and his prevarication. Usually we offer the client a cup of coffee and a little human sympathy, but there was a lot of telepathy passing between Stella and me today and she hadn't made a move toward the percolator. So I guessed she felt the same way.

'Do we get the address or are you going to sit there till fall,' I said.

Cramp winced like I'd struck him.

'Forgive me, Mr Faraday,' he said apologetically. 'We do a lot of work, indirectly, for the Museum of Ornithology.'

I blinked at him.

21

'Not the one here in L.A. You're not telling me their Curator goes in for exhibiting protected species that have only recently been shot.'

Cramp gave a really spectacular wince this time.

'Of course not, Mr Faraday,' he said stiffly. 'Please don't misunderstand me. We do a lot of discreet work for Vansittart Enterprises. We do the actual mounting and setting up of specimens. They do the plinths and engrave the plaques . . . '

'Don't go on,' I said. 'And present the Museum with a fifty per cent higher bill.'

Cramp shrugged.

'That's life, Mr Faraday. I could never get the Museum contract, unfortunately. The Curator doesn't like me.'

'I wonder why,' I said.

Cramp looked at me sharply. Stella buried her head in her notepad. I gave my client one of my bland looks. It must have worked because he sniffed and went on like I hadn't interrupted.

'It can be tough sometimes, Mr Faraday. Nobody knows. We do do work for various institutions, of course. I've always wanted the Museum contract but all the while Mr Van Horn has blocked me. There it is.'

'Pity,' I said. 'Especially as yours is the actual work which appears there.'

Cramp laid a finger alongside his nose.

'That's why it's such a discreet matter. I'd like Mr Vansittart approached very quietly.'

'I'll wear my slippers when I go see him,' I said.

Stella choked again and Cramp turned red. He was getting to look like a traffic signal by the minute.

'I'm sure you understand what I mean, Mr Faraday.'

'You can leave it to me,' I said. 'We'll get Vansittart's address from the book. You don't think he's responsible for this?'

Cramp shook his head.

'I shouldn't think so, Mr Faraday. He has the reputation for being a person of great probity. But there are many people in his establishment. And people do come and go there, of course.'

'I see what you mean,' I said. 'I'll look into it, Mr Cramp. You'll be hearing from me.'

Cramp got up and stood looking hesitantly at me.

'We still haven't gone into the matter of your rates, Mr Faraday.'

I gave them to him, both hourly and by the day. His face got longer and longer.

'It's a great deal of money,' he said.

'You can always call the police,' I said. 'I don't know why you haven't.'

He didn't rise to it, merely mumbled, 'I don't want to upset Mr Vansittart. And if the Museum gets to hear I mount up some of their specimens Van Horn would probably stop that too.'

I got his point.

'I see what you mean,' I said. 'Why not try the daily rate? It's cheaper.'

'The daily rate it is, Mr Faraday,' Cramp said earnestly.

He shook hands solemnly with Stella and then with me. He went out the office so quietly we hardly noticed it with the sun-dazzle through the blinds. But Stella was still smiling five minutes after he'd gone down in the elevator.

* * *

Stella put the coffee down on my blotter and sat back at her own desk. I sipped thankfully, looking at the client's chair which still bore the imprint of Cramp's angular form.

'All suggestions gratefully received,' I said.

Stella buried her blonde head in her cupped hands, inhaling the aroma of her coffee.

'Lots of possibilities, Mike,' she said cautiously.

'Such as?' I said.

Stella lifted her head, her blue eyes absorbed and thoughtful.

'Like Mr Cramp says. Vansittart had the specimens. Anyone could have doctored them at his place.'

'That's true,' I said. 'But so could the people who shot and sold the birds in the first place.'

Stella wrinkled up her nose. It didn't diminish her looks any.

'You mean someone might have used that eagle as a container for hot jewellery?'

'It's been done before,' I said.

'But something went wrong,' Stella went on, developing the theme. 'They were put there temporarily but the stuff was sent for mounting before the thieves realised it.'

'It's a possibility,' I said. 'But a pretty wacky one.'

Stella gave me a long look over the rim of her cup.

'We're in a wacky business, Mike.'

I didn't argue with that.

She got up and went over to the filing cabinet. She came back with a brown cardboard folder and riffled around among its contents while she finished off her first cup.

'I've got the two latest police hot property lists, Mike. There's nothing here that fits.'

'Perhaps it's too hot even for that,' I said.

Stella stared at me with approval. I pushed my cup across the blotter as she got up again. She went over to the alcove for a re-fill, came back and sat down. I rooted around in the biscuit tin, conscious of Stella's disapproving look.

She put the file back and busied herself

with the L.A. directory.

'Vansittart's place is 109–115 Shrimpton Boulevard,' she said.

'I know the section,' I said.

I scribbled the address down on the back of an envelope and put it back in my pocket. I glanced at my watch. It was already after four. I'd maybe look over there on my way home. Or maybe not. It was one of those days.

'I'm still listening,' I said.

'Suppose the stuff isn't stolen, Mike. What then?'

'I don't get you,' I said. 'It has to be. Otherwise, why would anyone want to ram all that stuff down that unfortunate bird's gullet?'

Stella smiled.

'It was dead already,' she reminded me.

'I should hope so,' I said. 'Otherwise we'd be getting the S.P.C.A. in on the case as well.'

Stella ignored that.

'You mustn't forget the Museum of Ornithology, Mike.'

'I'd never even given it a thought,' I said.

Stella shook her head disapprovingly.

'That stuff ended up there, didn't it?'

I stared at her for a long moment.

'The exhibits, I mean,' she went on.

'I know what you mean, honey,' I said. 'No need to build up too many theories until we've got something to go on.'

'Well, you won't find out by sitting here,' Stella said.

She glanced at her watch significantly.

'And you did say it had been a rough quarter.'

'I thought maybe I'd look over at Vansittart's,' I said.

Stella looked at her watch again.

'It's twenty after four already,' she said.

I took the hint, got up from the desk and drained my cup.

'Slave-driver,' I said. 'I'm on my way.'

Stella's smile lasted me all the way down to the ground floor.

3

Vansittart Enterprises Inc. had a set-up on Shrimpton Boulevard that was about as long as the Queen Mary. When I had a chance to look in its windows I found it was just as plushy too. In its heyday, of course. Not at the Long Beach location. I found a parking slot for the Buick and bruised my bumpers a bit while I was tooling in. I gave the big cop with the surly scowl one of my best smiles and walked back down to where the bronze and chrome building with the fancy red and white striped awnings sat.

The sun was so hot on the back of my grey lightweight that I could feel a big patch of sweat spreading before I'd gone a hundred yards. But it made a change from my last case where it hadn't stopped raining from beginning to end. Still, that's the P.I. business. It's all one thing or the other. With very little of the other. My joke lasted me all the way into the shade of the sun-blinds.

There were a lot of people about this afternoon on the sidewalks and most of them seemed to be staring in Vansittart's windows. I must say they were impressive. The first one I looked at had a carefully arranged landscape of tropical foliage with a real live stream running through it. Leastways, it was real live running water and it looked better than a real stream with its sparkling rivulets, big stones scattered about and the real grass bending in the artificial breeze that must have been coming from fans somewhere.

There were birds with vivid plumage, presumably wired to the rocking branches and lots of wild-life frozen in carefully simulated positions. It was all right if you liked that sort of thing. I didn't. I like to see real animals in the flesh, running live and free, but I had to admit it was beautifully done and uncannily realistic.

I wandered down a little farther. The next window was meant to be a winter landscape at sundown, with a setting sun in rear and very striking modelled mountains. In the foreground were a fox, a pine-marten and a timber-wolf. Again the modelling was superbly done. I was up by the main entrance now. That was a sort of arcade fronted by a steel grille that was now drawn back.

Beyond, the marble tiled floor led to the showroom entrance proper and there were glass cases down each side, illuminated and containing specimens of animal and bird-life set in their natural habitat. I didn't waste any more time on the exhibits. They began to pall a bit when one realised living creatures had to be killed in their prime to make such a display.

I went on in and paused by a gilded metal plaque. It had inscribed on it in gold lettering: VANSITTART ENTERPRISES. Wildlife Experts. Exhibits Prepared For Museum Display and For Private Collectors. I set fire to a cigarette and feathered out blue smoke. A wealthy-looking couple were just going through the main double doors so I followed on their heels. A carillon played somewhere as we got inside.

The place seemed to be floored in mink and there were cases of specimens everywhere one looked. Every type of wild animal from timber-wolves to squirrels simpered, smirked or snarled from pedestals, glass cases or from shelves high up on the walls. There were glass counters which contained even more dead animals and men who looked like stuffed exhibits themselves walked about warily in black cutaway coats, like secretary birds.

I avoided the nearest and went down the far end to where a tall blonde girl was thoughtfully brushing the coat of a pine-marten which was prancing about on a varnished teak stand.

She was quite something. She was about five feet ten in height, nicely built, with a willowy look about her. Her shimmering hair was pulled back in a pony-tail and glistened with health. She was about twenty-eight I would have said. She had steady grey eyes, affording a contrast to her hair and she had a broad, smooth brow and a lightly tanned skin that glowed with health too.

She wore a rust-coloured silk outfit that

looked like a pyjama suit to me, the trousers flared out, giving her a slightly nautical look. Her fingernails were pale pink and she had a gold brooch shaped like a butterfly that was pinned to the right-hand lapel of her jacket.

A pale blue silk scarf was thrust casually into the vee of her open-neck shirt and a black leather belt fitted tautly over her flat waist, emphasising the fullness of her breasts. Altogether she was one of the nicest things I'd seen for years. And the last thing I'd expected to see in a place like Vansittart Enterprises. She turned with a half smile as I came up and appraised me frankly.

'What can I do for you?'

Her voice was low and well-modulated.

'Quite a lot, I should imagine,' I said.

Her eyes were dancing with amusement now as she went on looking at me.

'I'll take a rain-check on it,' she said calmly, turning her attention back to the pine-marten. She continued brushing the shining coat of the animal carefully. It stared back at her with glazed eyes. I felt rather the same way myself.

'You're quite the liveliest thing in here,' I said.

She turned the steady grey eyes back on to me.

'I wouldn't have quite said that, Mr . . . ?'

'Faraday,' I said. 'What's yours?'

'Karen,' the blonde number said absently. 'Karen King. I'm a junior partner here.'

'That must be nice for the senior partner,' I said.

Once again a faint smile flowered at the corners of her mouth.

'I haven't had any complaints from him,' she said.

'I should think not,' I said gallantly.

I looked round at the serried ranks of silent animal figures that stretched from where we were standing to what seemed like the far horizon.

'Is he an animal lover too?'

The girl grinned this time and put the brush down on the glass-topped counter.

'I get your point, Mr Faraday. I take it you don't approve of dead animal specimens. In which case, why did you come here?'

'A good question,' I said. 'I'd like a

quiet word, Miss King, if you have somewhere private we can go.'

'Sure.'

The girl looked at the gold and diamond watch clamped to her wrist.

'I usually take some mint-tea around this time of the afternoon.'

'I'm not really a mint-tea type,' I said. 'But I'll gladly sit and watch you drink it.'

There were small dimples at the corners of the girl's mouth now. I could have stood and watched them all day.

'I must admit you don't look like a mint-tea man, Mr Faraday. But I think we can find you an ordinary brew if you'd care to join me.'

I grinned.

'Accepted in the gracious spirit in which it was offered, Miss King.'

★ ★ ★

The girl led the way down the big salon so fast that I almost had a job to keep up with her. On the way she was button-holed by a grim-looking woman with ashen-grey hair, who wore a severely cut suit to match her expression. She looked like the Joe Stalin Girl Commissar of the Month poster and didn't do anything for me.

She looked at me suspiciously as I loitered, waiting for the blonde number, and then walked swiftly into an inner office. The girl smiled apologetically.

'The tea will be along in a minute or two. Don't be put off by Miss Parker. She's got a delightful personality when you get to know her.'

'She must be a master of disguise,' I said.

The girl's façade almost broke up but not quite. She was too well-bred for that.

She led the way through a heavy oak door in rear of the salon which opened on to an elegant suite of offices, panelled in some blond wood that gave the place an opulent eighteenth century look. There were some expensive oil paintings on the walls which reinforced the initial impression; one or two discreet examples of Vansittart's art on polished stands; file-cabinets disguised by hand-made joinery got up to look like antique-work;

and a handsome desk that was surfaced with green, gold-tooled leather.

That looked like genuine eighteenth century too. Leastways, I've never seen modern walnut like it. They've lost the art nowadays. The girl went to sit in a carved armchair behind the desk and looked at me pensively. I was saved from any further dialogue by the phone buzzing. That was a mock-antique handset made in brass but with excellent taste. I expected it to be Madame Pompadour ordering some scones and toast to be sent to her room but it was only an inquiry from the salon because the King number referred it to someone else and said she wasn't to be disturbed for the next half-hour.

The door opened before she'd put the phone down and the Parker woman wheeled in carrying a silver tray. Up close she looked even more forbidding than before. She gave me a curt nod of the head, put the tray on the desk in front of the King girl and stood glowering until she put the phone down.

'You won't forget that Mancini order,'

she said in response to the query in the girl's eyes.

'I'm not likely to,' the girl said.

The Parker woman nodded and closed her mouth into such a thin line it looked like something on a sales graph.

'Just so long as I'm sure,' she said in a harsh voice.

I stared at her sharply. For a moment it almost sounded as though she were the employer and the girl the employee. Karen King evidently thought so too, because her eyes flickered to me and then back to the woman in the mannish suit. The Parker woman wasn't abashed but just stood her ground, staring steadily at the slim girl behind the desk. A slight flush was burning on her cheeks now.

'I think you can leave it to me, Miss Parker,' she said at last, in a low, placatory tone.

The woman nodded ponderously.

'Let us hope you are right,' she said frostily.

She went out with a heavy tread. I looked at the girl inquiringly.

'What was all that about?' I said.

Karen King was flushing now. She started pouring tea to cover her confusion.

'A rather delicate matter, Mr Faraday.'

I studied the woman's receding back. It was so square it looked like a brick wall disappearing through the door.

'What does she do around here?' I asked.

The girl got up to hand me the tea. I went over and took the cup from her.

'She has a sort of roving commission,' she said. 'It's rather ambiguous really and sometimes causes minor difficulties.'

'So I should imagine,' I said.

I sat down in a green leather padded chair that the girl indicated. The door clicked in the silence like the Parker woman had been listening behind it. It was quiet and restful in here, after the bustle and heat of L.A.

'A roving commission for whom?' I said.

The girl shrugged.

'For Mr Vansittart.'

Her eyes slowly widened, as though with surprise.

'I don't really know why I'm telling you all this, Mr Faraday.'

'Because I'm such a charming person,' I said.

The King girl burst out laughing and sat staring at me for a long moment.

'You're very cool, at any rate,' she said.

'It's my upbringing,' I said. 'I didn't mean to be rude, but you're the junior partner and it looked like she was trying to give you orders.'

The girl tapped with her spoon on the edge of the cup.

'It often looks like that to outsiders, Mr Faraday,' she said softly. 'Every fairly large business has its drawbacks.'

'Miss Parker being one of them?' I said.

The girl smiled faintly and picked up her cup.

'That's not for me to say, Mr Faraday. But I leave you to judge.'

I nodded, picking up my own cup. The tea was really good. I'm no great judge and I don't drink a lot of it but this had been made by someone who knew what he or she was doing.

'This is really excellent,' I said, and meant it.

The girl looked at me with approval.

'I'm glad you like it, Mr Faraday. It's a special blend. We get it from a Chinese wholesaler on the other side of town.'

'And Miss Parker brews it?' I said.

The girl shook her head.

'Not Miss Parker,' she said softly. 'She's hardly the type.'

I let it go. She had a point there though. We drank in silence for a few moments longer, the cogs of my mind revolving swiftly. I hadn't quite worked out my tactics but the girl was making it easier for me. I guess it must have been her slack afternoon and I was one way of passing her time. Though I wondered why she bothered with me. She couldn't have been short of admirers.

'I expect you wonder why I'm here,' I said after a discreet interval.

Karen King put her cup down with a faint chinking noise in the silence.

'The thought had crossed my mind,' she said.

'This might take a few minutes,' I said.

The girl shrugged.

'That's what we're here for, Mr Faraday. As long as it's about taxidermy.'

I looked at her calm grey eyes and the shimmering blonde hair, my thoughts a long way from the subject.

'It's about taxidermy,' I said.

4

I lit a cigarette and feathered out blue smoke at the ceiling. Karen King got up and came over with the silver tea-pot. She took my cup, shook out the dregs in a silver bowl, poured in fresh milk and had the silver-handled strainer over the cup before you could say P.G. Wodehouse. I sat and watched the golden liquid descending into the cup feeling like I had somehow strayed into a thirties movie. That was the effect Karen King had on me.

I thanked her and she went back the other side of the desk. She sat down and looked at me with a dreamy expression in her eyes.

'You're an unusual man, Mr Faraday.'

'In what way?' I said.

She made an abrupt little movement in her big chair like I'd caught her off guard.

'In many ways. I've been studying you closely. You're not at all the sort of person who usually has a call on our services.'

'You're right there at least,' I said, tapping off the ash from my cigarette in a crystal tray at the edge of the girl's desk. Karen King sat silent, pouring herself another cup of the mint tea. I could catch the fresh, slightly acrid aroma right from where I was sitting.

I had to choose my words with care. I couldn't afford to make a mistake with this girl. I wanted to find out something about Vansittart without arousing her suspicions. I figured it was going to be difficult.

'I've got a little problem,' I said. 'I figured you might be able to help.'

The girl put down the teapot with a flowing, eloquent movement and sat with her small, pink-nailed hands folded on the elegant green leather surface of the desk.

'Like I said, that's why we're here, Mr Faraday.'

She sounded like me, in my own office. I paused, holding her eyes with my own.

'I wondered if I might ask you a few technical questions?'

There was wariness in the eyes now.

'I'm sure you'll forgive me for asking, Mr Faraday, but you're not in the business yourself by any chance?'

I stopped, looking at her in surprise. Then I saw what she meant. I grinned, shaking my head.

'Nothing like that, Miss King. I'm not a rival, trying to steal your secrets, if that's what you mean.'

The girl shifted again in her chair.

'Hardly anything so crude as that, Mr Faraday. But the thought had crossed my mind.'

'I'm sorry,' I said. 'I should have provided some identification.'

I gave her my driver's licence. I didn't want her to know what my business was, so I couldn't give her one of our official cards. But the licence identified me and gave my address. The girl stared at it in silence, her eyes narrowed a little. But it satisfied her all right, because she relaxed after a moment and handed it back to me with a graceful little gesture of her hand.

'That seems perfectly satisfactory, Mr Faraday. It's a nice spot, Park West.'

'It's all right,' I said. 'It gets the fresh air from time to time.'

The girl's eyes were still curious.

'You're taking a long time to come to the point, Mr Faraday.'

'I'll get right to it,' I said. 'I have a friend who's a great collector. He lives in San Francisco but he's thinking of moving to L.A. He asked me who the best people in the area were for mounting specimens. I looked you up and thought I'd come along to see for myself.'

The girl had completely relaxed now, her eyes shifting from my face.

'I expect you think we all say that, Mr Faraday, but you couldn't come to a better place. There are some half-dozen people in the L.A. basin who are really outstanding in the business. We're among the top three, I'd say.'

'And expensive?' I said.

The girl nodded, smiling faintly.

'We don't come cheap, Mr Faraday. But then high quality never does.'

She hesitated, her eyes searching my face.

'You didn't say what sort of collector

your friend was.'

'I'm sorry,' I said. 'Small game animals and rare birds mostly.'

The girl looked at me approvingly.

'There doesn't seem to be any problem. I can give you one of our brochures and any further information you may require.'

'Fine,' I said. 'You do deal with rare birds, I take it?'

'Of course, Mr Faraday,' the girl said softly. 'In fact we deal with most things, except the really big mammals. They take too much time and are too specialised even for us. Museums usually have their own resident staff to deal with those.'

'I see,' I said. 'I shouldn't think there would be anything bigger than small deer.'

'Excellent,' the girl said.

Her grey eyes drifted across to me and then focused with startling sharpness.

'You didn't say whether your friend was a private person or represented an institution.'

'Oh, private,' I said. 'But he's in a big way of collecting. I figure he could

47

provide you with a good deal of work. I wondered if it would be possible to have a look round some time. I'd like to give him a first-hand report.'

The girl looked at me with a dubious expression at the back of her eyes.

'It's a little unusual, Mr Faraday, but it might be arranged.'

She was smiling now.

'We close in half an hour. If you'd care to hang around I'll give you a personal guided tour.'

I looked at her glowing face across the desk.

'I'll hang around, Miss King,' I said.

★ ★ ★

'This is where most of the highly-skilled work is done, Mr Faraday,' Karen King said.

She glided down the big work-room in front of me, the powerful overhead lamps shimmering on the golden mass of her hair. There was the sharp, pungent smell of chemicals in the air. The place had been closed some little while and the only sound was the faint hum of a vacuum cleaner as a white-coated woman polished the show-room floor. Apart from three or four cleaners we seemed to be the only people in the building right now.

'It seems a fascinating process,' I said, bringing up in front of a glass-fronted cupboard, where a lot of lethal-looking instruments glinted in the harsh light. Karen King grinned mockingly.

'You're an excellent liar, Mr Faraday,' she said amiably. 'You're not really interested in taxidermy at all, are you?'

I looked at her thoughtfully.

'I never pretended otherwise, Miss King. Like I said I'm here on behalf of a friend.'

She licked her full lips with the tip of a very pink tongue.

'Well, I hope you're suitably impressed on his behalf?'

'I am, I am,' I said. 'And it's good for you to take so much trouble for a stranger.'

I hesitated, listening to a faint sound like that made by a furtively closing door in the middle distance.

49

'You're sure Miss Parker's not still around?'

The girl shook her head.

'She went soon after we had tea. She's gone out to Mr Vansittart's to make a report. Does she worry you?'

I shook my head.

'Not really. Except she's got the build of an all-in wrestler. I wouldn't like to mix it with her.'

Karen King showed perfect teeth as she laughed.

'Do you always judge women by whether they're likely to last ten rounds with you?'

I shook my head.

'Not all women. Only selected specimens.'

The girl stood back from me and put her hands on her hips. She looked great like that and I could have watched her all evening.

'What category do you place me in, Mr Faraday?'

'First-grade, Miss King,' I said. 'I wouldn't want to wrestle with you. Not in that sense anyway.'

The girl made a little mock-grimace.

'That's disappointing, Mr Faraday,' she said softly.

We were standing quite close together and suddenly she was in my arms. We were kissing quite a long time and I'm not usually very over-heated about such things but I could have sworn we levitated to about a foot above the floor. When we came down again there was a singing in my ears. I never could stand altitudes.

'Very nice indeed,' I said. 'No complaints I hope?'

The girl pushed herself gently away.

'No complaints, Mr Faraday. You want to continue with the tour or shall we call it a day?'

'I could go on all night,' I said.

The King number gurgled quietly to herself.

'I was talking about business,' she said. 'You were going to report to your friend about the mysteries of taxidermy.'

'I was?' I said.

The girl put her hand flat against my chest and gently held me off as I tried to move toward her again.

'That will do, Mr Faraday. It was just a sample.'

'When can we sample some more?' I said.

The girl shook her head, her white teeth glinting in her tanned face.

'We'll take a rain-check on it. We're both busy people. What would Mr Vansittart think if he came in and found us like this?'

'You didn't care what Vansittart thought just now,' I said. 'Besides, I thought you said he was at home.'

The girl smiled faintly and moved off down the room. I followed, my pulse still racing a little.

'He is, Mr Faraday, so far as I know,' she said.

I was back on track again.

'I wonder if it's the same person my friend knew in San Francisco,' I said. 'I seem to remember him speaking about a Vansittart in connection with taxidermy.'

I was talking purely off the top of my head but the girl considered it silently for a moment or two. We were back in the main show-room now. Two white-coated women were working among the show-cases and counters with vacuum-cleaners with special attachments. They took no notice of us, just went on with their cleaning, like we didn't exist. They reminded me of a B-movie I'd once seen about zombies.

'Mr Vansittart did have connections in San Francisco,' she said thoughtfully.

'A big man with a heavy mustache?' I said.

I was striking out in the dark but once again I won the kewpie doll. The girl nodded.

'That's him, Mr Faraday.'

'I wonder if you could give me his private address?' I said. 'I'd just like to have a word with him as well if that's in order.'

The girl raised her eyebrows.

'I can't see any objection. Though he may not like being disturbed at home.'

'I'll maybe give him a ring first,' I said.

The girl led the way over to the nearest glass counter.

'There's no secret about it. It's on our business cards.'

She picked up the big oblong of pasteboard which had gold-printed deckle edges. I glanced at the legend in the centre; it had Vansittart's name and address down in the bottom right-hand corner as principal director. It had a couple of other names in the centre, who looked like they might have been sleeping partners, because no addresses were given. The girl's name and address were in the left-hand corner. I looked at her sidewise.

'I'll hang on to this,' I said. 'And thanks.'

Karen King stood, slim, decorative and self-assured, regarding me from under half-closed eyelids.

'Come out and question me some evening,' she said. 'I'm home most nights.'

'I'll take a rain-check on that too,' I said.

She walked me over to the main doors and held out her hand formally.

'Good night, Mr Faraday. It's been a pleasure.'

'Mutual,' I said.

She unlocked the door for me and re-locked it behind me. I went out and down the boulevard feeling like I was walking a couple of inches above the sidewalk.

I got back to the Buick and lit a cigarette while I tuned the radio to a news bulletin. I glanced at the card again and put it down on the passenger seat at my side. I sat smoking quietly and thinking things over. Not that I had much to think over. But Cramp's little problem kept gnawing at my mind. Or what's left of it after years of stake-out and investigating people's grubby little problems.

I had no doubt Stella's estimate of around 150,000 dollars-worth value on those jewels was about right. The fact that no such haul was mentioned on recent stolen property sheets didn't mean anything. I guessed they'd have been stolen all right. The two most intriguing aspects of the situation were the method employed to hide the items; and why they should have been stuffed in a dead eagle's crop at all.

The fact that such birds were on the

protected list and therefore illegal to kill and collect didn't help at all; it just made things more tricky when dealing with someone like Vansittart. I didn't think the girl knew anything about the situation at all. Like Cramp had said Vansittart handled that side personally.

But Vansittart must have known the deal was shaky; according to Cramp he'd done a lot of illegal work like that for him. Question was, had Vansittart or one of his employees put the stuff in there? Or had it happened at the place where the birds were killed? In which case I had to go to Vansittart to find out their source. Which would be tricky too.

I could have asked the girl to look up the records, of course. But that wouldn't have got me anywhere. It would have tipped my hand straight away. Like I'd told Cramp I had to act cautiously. I figured I'd probably rely on my non-existent friend in San Francisco.

By a lucky chance I'd hit on the right description of Vansittart. That authenticated the situation with the girl; though she might still ring the senior partner to warn him I was coming out. I'd ask Vansittart about the situation over protected birds, man to man. That might open up something because Vansittart probably charged a premium for such work; according to Cramp he did it on quite a scale.

And the San Francisco angle would let Cramp off the hook. The more I thought about it the more I liked it. Not that it was particularly brilliant; but it was all I had for the moment. Vansittart was the man I had to see. He was the only one who could give me a possible address from which the specimens had originated. I sat on, finishing my cigarette, listening to the tail-end of the bulletin, the sun comfortably warm on my back and gleaming off the windshield.

I had the windows open and there was a cooling breeze coming through, dispelling the smog and the grit and bringing with it the cloying perfume of tropical flowers which helped to damp down the gasoline fumes. L.A. was a great place if you didn't let it throw you.

I finished off my cigarette, ground out

the butt in the dashboard tray and started the motor. I glanced at Vansittart's address again and tooled out into the seething stream of traffic.

5

It took me about an hour to get out there. I wondered why Vansittart had such an elaborate set-up in back of his salon. I'd no doubt he'd been a skilful taxidermist in his time. But like many people he'd found there was more money to be made in farming out the hard graft to a reliable man like Cramp and skimming off the cream at the top end. I guessed he had staff on hand still who did a certain amount of preparation and mounting of specimens.

He would have to have, to satisfy clients who thought all the work was done on his own premises. Which brought in once more the question of whether some underling on Vansittart's staff had hidden the jewellery. The more I thought about it the crazier it seemed. No inquiries had been made of Cramp, of course. That was significant. One would have expected something if the people at Vansittart's place were responsible.

Because they would have missed the stuff straight away. Not to mention the fact that they would know the two birds in question were going out to Cramp's. On reflection I dismissed that theory. That left only the possibility that the jewellery had originated with the people who'd left the birds with Vansittart. Which was crazier still, because they'd also know the stuff would be found in the eagle's crop.

I gave up beating my brains out and concentrated on the driving. It was tricky going up into the hills and I settled down to the hairpins, enjoying the dying of the sun against the darker blue of the peaks and the cooler rush of the air up here. I reached Pine Ridge Canyon in good time and idled on down, looking for the turn I wanted.

Several cars were coming down the canyon and I had to wait for a few seconds to cross. I tooled on up, relishing the coolness of the breeze and the mellow light which glimmered on the green and pink tiles of the houses and the greenness of the closely shaved turf which was kept that way only through virtue of the very expensive and constantly used sprinkler systems.

Vansittart's was a very big spread on two levels, using lots of local stone from the canyon with teak and cedar cladding. It was a cross between a ranch and a Swiss chalet and must have cost a lot of money. More than I could have afforded in a life-time of gum-shoe work. I drifted my heap up a drive floored with pink-gravel and ground it to a halt beside a beige Alfa-Romeo that made my five-year-old powder-blue Buick look like something out of a Christmas cracker. It's another world, Mike, I told myself.

There was a four-car garage on a lower level at the left-hand side of the house with the doors standing open; a lot of flowering trees that were coming into full-bloom; and a big verandah that ran the whole length of the house on the top floor, that looked like it opened off on to bedrooms.

I could hear a mower going in the near distance and I walked on a crazy paved

61

path a little way round the house to where a Japanese gardener in a wide-brimmed floppy white hat was manicuring the turf and swearing to himself in his own language. He listened impassively while I explained my presence there and gestured up toward the front of the house.

'Mr Vansittart inside,' he said. 'You tell him I need new machine.'

'We all have our problems,' I told him.

I left him there and went back along the path and around to the front of the mansion. I went up some zig-zag steps across the stepped garden and got on to the lower terrace surrounding the house. The ornate front door was standing wide open, propped back with a heavy brass Buddha ornament and I pulled the bell-rope, listening to its heavy jangle somewhere in the interior. Nothing stirred and there was no sound apart from the distant noise of the mower and the nervous chitter of bird-song.

Nothing happened for about five minutes and I hit the bell again. I was still standing there when the mower stopped. Then a more irritating noise began. It came from a two-stroke motor and a few seconds later the Japanese came whining and snorting up the path on one of those low-powered motor-cycles whose engines tear at the nerves. He waved at me jauntily, the machine swerved and he almost took a header into one of the ornamental bushes; then he had control again and went thrudding into the distance, the bruised silence slowly and painfully crawling back in.

I was getting tired of standing there so I stepped into the cool shadowiness of the entrance hall. The place was extravagantly got up with heavy oil-paintings in gilt frames; Second Empire tables; and sporting prints which floated against the thick silk wallpaper. I went on through into a living room that must have been all of eighty feet long. It had magnificent views of the valley beyond through the big picture windows but I had no time for that either.

There was an archway over at the left-hand side which had an oval door built within it. I went on into Vansittart's study which was another big room lined with leather-bound volumes. There was a lot of stuff on company law, taxidermy and ornithology, and a few classics interspersed. The books looked as though they had been read and studied too. Which is something in California where executives often buy books by the yard to use as shelf furniture.

I took one or two of the taxidermy volumes down; there was no doubt Vansittart knew his stuff because there were inked annotations in the margins of some of them, with an occasional acid comment indicating disagreement here and there. I put them back and went back in the living room. There was a heavy silence now that the noise of the mower had stopped and the sun declining behind the low hills gave the place a melancholy it hadn't had when I'd first arrived.

I went back over toward the entrance hall, calling Vansittart's name. Nothing stirred anywhere. There were a number of other doors opening off the hall but I didn't try them. I went halfway up the big curving white staircase and again called Vansittart's name.

Again there was no response but I could hear the faint fret of water running now. I went up another couple of treads. It was clearer. It sounded like Vansittart might be taking a bath. Whether he was alone or not I would have to risk. I went on up, listening to the running water, my mind full of unspoken thoughts about eagles and taxidermy.

★ ★ ★

It didn't take me long to locate the source of the noise. There was a big master bedroom at the head of the stairs, whose door was standing wide open. I went on in. The bathroom was en suite and opened up at the right-hand side. I knocked at the door but there was no response. I knew it was the bathroom because the noise of the water was obviously coming from there. I tried the handle.

The door was unlocked and I went on through into a pink-tiled apartment which had lots of mirrors; matching double washbasins; a low-level toilet suite; and matching bidet. The bath was oyster-shaped with gold-plated taps. It was empty but full of water. The cold-tap had been left running and the water draining out the overflow had been making the noise.

I went over and turned the tap off and then took out the main plug and drained the bath. It was an impertinence in another man's house but I figured it would be an economy in the long run because I was saving water. Besides, the sound was getting on my nerves.

I went back into the bedroom and across to the window. I could see the whole of the garden spread out here. It was about two acres in extent and the lie of the land was such that I could see it was empty. Unless Vansittart, bathrobe and all, was sitting in one of the small pagodas and suntraps that were scattered about the paths that bordered a small ornamental lake up at the far end.

There was the obligatory pool too but that was on the terrace below me and there was no-one in the cane chairs that surrounded it. I lit a cigarette and put the spent matchstalk back in the box, standing by the window, the dying sun warm on my cheek, blue smoke slowly ascending to the ceiling while I listened to the lonely pumping of my heart.

I came back down again in the end and went back through the ground floor rooms, including the kitchen. There was no-one around. Of course, Vansittart didn't have to be in his bathrobe. He could simply have gone for a walk in his own grounds. Or called on a neighbour for that matter. I guessed he wouldn't have gone far. If the Alfa belonged to him — and I guessed it did — then he was still around somewhere.

The house itself and the silence was beginning to get on my nerves. I went back upstairs again, a tiny muscle twitching in my cheek. That was an infallible sign to me that there was something wrong. I went through the top of the house. There were several other bedrooms, two of them with their own bathrooms; a sun-room and what looked like a play-room which had a couple of table-tennis tables; a billiard table; and an elaborate model railway set out on benches. I could have played with it all evening but that wasn't why I was here.

By the time I'd got through I was certain there was something wrong. I went back into the bathroom again. I sat on the edge of the bath and finished my cigarette and puzzled things out. Not that there was much to puzzle out. When one was pointed in the right direction, that is. That was when I spotted the wet foot-marks on the tiled floor. Leastways, they had been wet but the warm air had almost dried them out. They started by the edge of the bath and went over toward the door. They died out halfway across. I bent down and studied them more closely. They were the prints of bare feet; the ball of the feet and the toes only, like their owner had been walking on tip-toe.

I straightened up, the hairs on the nape of my neck making a small tickling sensation. I stood there in the heavy silence, the muscle twitching in my cheek again. There was something badly wrong here; I'd been too long at the game not to know the symptoms. But I wasn't quite ready for it yet.

It was a beautiful day and I didn't want to spoil it. Not for the moment. So I went over to the window again, finished off my cigarette. When I'd done that I crushed it out carefully on the inside of the package and put the butt back. I knew enough not to leave such things around.

I went into the bedroom. There were big wardrobes with sliding doors in here. I opened them up, went through them. There was a lot of expensive suiting and custom-built shoes in them. Plus a section which had women's dresses and underwear. I didn't touch anything, just opened the doors and looked. I came back into the bathroom and stood listening to the heavy silence of the house. A tap dripped insistently in one of the basins. The sound got on my nerves after a while and I went over and turned it off. The thin thread of water died and with it, the sound.

I stopped to look at the imprints of the feet once more. There was no doubt about them. I was at a slightly different angle now. I noticed for the first time a low, white-painted stool at the far end of the oyster-shaped bath. I hadn't seen it before because it had been in shadow. There was a red silk dressing-gown carefully folded on top of it. A pair of men's slippers were tucked in beneath the stool.

I went over to the large cupboard at the far side of the bathroom. Like I figured it was for linen and had pipes running through it to dry the stuff out. It was a big cupboard with shelves at the top. Someone had turned the key in the lock and I had a job to unlock it. There was a weight pressing against the door which made it difficult.

So I wasn't too surprised when the naked body of a big man with a black mustache who could only have been the late Mr Vansittart came out with an obscene rush and sprawled in all the squalid ugliness of death on the elegant tiled floor.

6

It was quite a moment, all the same. I stepped back and looked down at the corpse. I couldn't see any sign of a wound or any obvious cause of death. But it was certain he hadn't locked himself in the cupboard from the outside. Which ruled out suicide in my book. Or anyone else's for that matter.

I wished for a moment that the Japanese gardener hadn't taken off. Not that I suspected him. But he could have provided an alibi for me. And he'd had a good look at me. Come to that Karen King knew I was coming out here. I wondered what had happened to the Parker woman. She'd probably arrived, couldn't get any reply to her ringing and gone away again. I remembered then the stream of cars which were coming off the bluff. The gardener could have told me about that as well.

I sat down on the edge of the bath

again and lit another cigarette. I was getting to be quite a heavy smoker on this case. I had to play things carefully. On the other hand the gardener might not remember me very clearly; he'd looked a little myopic to me. It was a big might though. And equally he might or might not have remembered the number of my heap. Though I could still say I'd kept on ringing and no-one had come. So I'd gotten tired and gone away.

The more I thought about it the more I liked it. It was the only way to play it. If I wanted to keep my name out of the papers. Otherwise it would tip my hand to anyone interested in high-class jewellery, stuffed eagles and murder. I had no doubt that all these things were connected. It was too much for coincidence. I couldn't prove murder, of course. Not without an autopsy.

I got up again and looked down at Vansittart. There was something curious about the head. I got a towel from the edge of the bath and gently pushed it. It rolled over at a grotesque angle to the body. The neck had been broken. I could see the big bluish-green bruise now. Someone had given him the father of all karate chops as he ran across the bathroom floor.

I wondered if his firm would have him mounted and put in a glass case down at Karen King's show-rooms. A fly buzzed suddenly in the empty silence. That wasn't very funny, Mike, I told myself. But it was all I had in the way of light relief this afternoon. I decided not to hang around any longer. Vansittart might have a girl-friend or staff due back any minute.

I went and put the towel on the edge of the bath, checked to make sure I hadn't left any of my own footprints in a damp patch on the tiling anywhere. I couldn't see anything. I put my hand on the body before I left. It was still warm. That meant he'd been killed only about half an hour or so before I arrived. So the gardener had to know who did it.

Unless the killer had come across the grounds at the back while the Japanese was occupied somewhere else. Which was entirely feasible. The garden was a big place and anyone could easily have come in through the open front door and left the same way without being seen. If they were careful, of course. And providing they'd left their automobile some way down the road. Which they would have done. In both cases.

I carefully dispersed my tobacco-smoke and went on out the bathroom, walking quietly like it was a chapel of rest or something. It was the next worst thing this evening. I got down to the front porch and glanced around. There was nobody about but there was aural evidence of activity in the gardens adjoining; a high, thin cry like that of a young child; a couple of mowers competing for attention; and a low, toneless singing interspersed with the clack of hedge-cutting shears.

I went down the front path of the house feeling like I was on a lighted stage. Nothing moved in the brilliance and shimmering heat. I could feel clammy patches of sweat in the small of my back and under my armpits. I walked back to where I'd left the Buick next the beige

Alfa-Romeo. I slid behind the wheel, wincing as the heat from the upholstery seared my back. It was then I saw a small blurred patch of white from the corner of my eye.

It moved as I focused up on it. The old lady under the yellowing straw bonnet was poised by her hedge, staring at me suspiciously through steel-rimmed spectacles. She had on heavy duty wash-leather gloves and she held the heavy pair of steel secateurs halfway between her body and the hedge like she had paused in mid-stroke when I walked out.

I put up my arm across my face like I was shielding it from the sun. She was a good way away so I hoped her eyes wouldn't be sharp enough to read the licence plate details of my heap. One never can tell with old ladies. But it would be stupid to let her identify my face if she was unable to read the number plate. I forced myself to sit there for what seemed like an age.

Then the steady clack of the secateurs started again. I waited for a minute or so and then took my hand down from my eyes. The old lady had moved around the corner of her hedge and was back on her property, minding her own business. I started up the motor then. The sound seemed to wake the echoes all the way across the L.A. basin and back again.

I drove slowly down the drive but I didn't see her again. Then I went away quietly but fast, trying not to attract any attention. I didn't stop sweating until I was a couple of miles away.

★　★　★

Karen King lived in a plushy apartment block over on the other side of town. It took me three-quarters of an hour to get there. I parked in one of the reserved slots at the side of the building and thumbed my way up to the fourth floor. It was one of those chintzy set-ups where you can smell the folding money a mile away; from the expensive carpeting in the reception area to the limited edition prints in gold frames on the corridors leading to the apartments.

But I hadn't missed the small TV

cameras in the ceiling mountings and the discreet but unmistakable security precautions; from the bulge in the commissionaire's well-cut military-style jacket to the faint crackle of radio static. I guessed there would be a top-security room in the basement where the TV scanning material and video-tapes would be monitored; and armed guards staked out in rooms on every floor.

It was just another symptom of a sick society, and Southern California's in particular. Most plushy apartment blocks had this kind of security written into their expensive leases and the only reason I hadn't been challenged was probably because I looked reasonably respectable. I wasn't carrying the Smith-Wesson today; it hadn't been that sort of case — until now. But I guessed there would have been metal-detectors at work and I would have been challenged before I hit the elevator.

I mentally gave the management of the Florida Apartments a high rating as I walked down the long corridor, looking for 221B. I found it in the end, on a corner location which obviously would have balcony gardens overlooking two streets. I upped Karen King's status as I buttoned the bell. It would have cost me five years' earnings just to pay the rent here for a year.

'Yes?'

It was the girl's voice all right, coming out of a small chrome grille next the door.

'Faraday here, Miss King,' I said. 'I'd like to talk to you if you could spare me a few minutes.'

The voice sounded amused.

'You don't waste much time, Mr Faraday. I said 'some evening'. Not necessarily tonight.'

'This is urgent,' I said. 'It's nothing personal.'

'How disappointing,' Karen King said.

'Do I get to see you?' I said. 'I can't talk out here.'

'Of course, Mr Faraday.'

The door opened and the tall number stood there; she still wore the pyjama suit but she'd done something to her hair and make-up and she had a shiny new look about her that I found pretty fetching.

'Come on in.'

The girl paused, looking me over.

'I was going to throw a steak and salad together. It would be just as easy to prepare for two.'

I nodded, closing the door behind me.

'Thanks,' I said. 'It would suit me fine.'

The girl led the way across the hall to a big room which had a fine view of the city and the smog through the vast windows which gave on to the balcony.

'I was going to eat outside. I take it you've no objection.'

I shook my head.

'None at all.'

The girl passed a full tongue across her lower lip. She seemed to read my every thought.

'If you'd like to wash your hands, Mr Faraday, the bathroom's just across the hall. I'll be in the kitchen.'

I thanked her and went back into the hall again. The bathroom was where she said it was. My face stared back, dark and sardonic from the oval mirror set over a washbasin that seemed to be made of pure gold. I washed, combed my hair and straightened my tie. I looked quite reasonable by the time I'd fought my way back into the living room again.

It was typical Southern California apartment-style, but none the worse for that. Good original paintings on the walls; a vast stone fireplace that would never be used; genuine antique furniture. A large platform area for dining in winter. There were thousands of books, which I guessed would be the girl's. Most of the stuff was supplied by the management, but these wouldn't be.

I wandered up and down the shelves, selecting a volume here and there. They were good things too and looked like they had been read; ranging from Salinger to Tolstoy; from Leo Rosten to Italo Svevo. I raised my eyebrows once or twice. The girl poked her head round the jamb of a door leading off the platform area.

'If you'd like a drink there's Scotch in the bar. You'll find an ice-chest in back. I'd like a dry martini.'

'Coming up,' I said.

My eyes raked the room while I prepared the drinks. I didn't see anything out of the ordinary. When I'd finished I closed up the ice-chest and carried the stuff over toward the kitchen. It looked like something out of Star-Trek when I got inside. All stainless steel and electronics but the girl looked just as much at home there as in the show-room.

She took the drink from me, her eyes searching my face. I toasted her silently over the rim of my glass.

'You said you had something urgent to tell me.'

'It can wait a little,' I said. 'Now is hardly the time.'

'You mean it's not that urgent?'

The smooth brow beneath the blonde hair was suddenly crinkled with thought.

'Not exactly,' I said. 'But half-an-hour won't make much difference now.'

I tasted my drink. It was smooth and smoky, just like it should be.

'You're very enigmatic, Mr Faraday,' the girl said.

She went back over to the massive cooking-range and started doing things to sizzling steaks with long steel forks with bone handles. A very pleasant aroma was

81

starting to fill the place.

'You found Mr Vansittart all right?'

I stared into her eyes but I couldn't read anything in them but faint curiosity.

'Sure,' I said. 'I found him all right.'

I'd decided to level with her but I was still feeling my way. My only chance now of finding out where those specimens had come from lay with her. After tomorrow the place would be swarming with the law and they'd hardly be likely to tell me. Even if they knew what I was looking for.

She moved over to a pine-topped fixture and started chopping up materials for the salad. She was deft, efficient and elegant in everything she did.

'You can prepare the plates if you like,' she said.

'I'm the best salad thrower you ever saw,' I said.

Her smile lasted for quite half a minute. I could have stood and watched it all evening but I had other things on my mind tonight. When I'd finished with the salad I carried a tray-full of stuff out on to the balcony. That was pretty nice too and was got up with screens and trellis-work and lots of tropical foliage writhing out of teak-trunking set round the edges.

It was getting dark now and thousands of neons and other lights were beginning to prick the dusk and mingle with the pale fire of the sky as the light left it. There was a cool breeze up here and I took off my jacket and rolled up my sleeves. The girl came out while I was fixing the table, carrying the main course and what looked like an excellent bottle of Californian burgundy. And we do have some good ones, whatever the Europeans might think.

'As this seems to be something of an occasion,' she said.

She smiled gravely and went around the table, lighting red wax candles in protective shades. She went back over to a switch near the living room door and killed the balcony lights. We ate by the bloom of the candles which grew stronger as the daylight died from the sky. It was all right if you liked that sort of thing. I did and I don't get enough of it in my business.

She knew how to cook a steak too

which added to the pleasure of the occasion. We were on our second glass of wine before she spoke again. It was quite dark now, except for the neons below and the two candles on the table and her face was a pale oval as she studied me. She lifted her glass to touch the rim of my own and we drank silently. She put hers down on the cloth in front of her like she'd come to a decision.

'You aren't interested in taxidermy, Mr Faraday? And you haven't a friend in San Francisco who wants to commission us?'

I shook my head. She evinced no surprise.

'What are you, Mr Faraday?'

'A private detective,' I said.

I got out the photostat of my licence and showed it to her. There was shock in her eyes now but she controlled herself admirably. She put out a pink finger to flick an imaginary crumb of bread from off the cloth. It was an entirely automatic reaction while she adjusted to my information.

'I don't understand. What is your business with me?'

'Murder is my business,' I told her.

7

There was a silence so long and so deep that I wasn't even conscious of the faint roar of the traffic coming up from the street. Then Karen King picked up her glass and drained it. I poured her another. Her face was a pale oval in the soft light cast by the candles.

'I still don't understand, Mr Faraday. Murder? Whose murder?'

I leaned across the table toward her.

'I'm going to confide in you, Miss King. Principally because I need your help. But first I want your word that what I'm going to say won't go beyond this terrace.'

My last sentence was pretty flowery in both senses of the word but I wanted to spell things out as plainly as possible. The girl had set her mouth in a stubborn line. She looked great like that.

'Have you done something wrong, Mr Faraday?'

I shook my head.

'Nothing like that, I can assure you.'

The girl's eyes searched my face like she was looking for some reassurance there. She must have found it because she went on, almost dreamily, 'I only met you just today, Mr Faraday. Yet I feel I could trust you with almost anything.'

It was my turn to be surprised.

'It's good to hear you say so,' I said. 'You can. And I do mean that.'

The blonde girl reached out a long, slim hand and put it impulsively on my arm.

'I'm glad, Mr Faraday. I'm waiting to hear what the problem is.'

'I have your word?' I said.

She nodded, the dancing candle flames making little stipples of light on her face.

'You have.'

'All right, then,' I said. 'I was engaged by a client to find out something about some specimens Vansittart sent him for mounting up.'

The girl half-opened her mouth as if to say something but I stopped her with a quick gesture of my hand.

'No names, Miss King. We're talking about one of my anonymous clients.'

The girl shot me a brief smile.

'I get you, Mr Faraday.'

'I hope you do,' I said. 'Because this is an awkward business. I needed to question Vansittart about the source, which is why I visited your premises today.'

The girl's eyes were dark and enigmatic as she stared out across at the misty lights which powdered the horizon.

'To pump me?'

'If you like,' I said. 'But I really needed to reach Vansittart without arousing his suspicions.'

Again the girl made as though she meant to interrupt me but she kept her silence as I went on.

'All I wanted was the name and address of the people who'd sent the specimens to Vansittart. Apparently he handled them in strict secrecy.'

The girl's face was alive with interest now.

'Why would he do that, Mr Faraday?'

'Because the specimens were prohibited birds, which had been shot illegally.'

Karen King's mouth was a round O of surprise.

'You're sure of that, Mr Faraday?'

'As sure as I'm sitting here,' I said.

I shot her a sharp glance.

'You didn't know anything about it?'

The girl tossed her blonde hair angrily.

'Too damned true I didn't. Why would Vansittart want to do such things?'

'For millionaire clients,' I said. 'For money, of course.'

The girl's face was a mask of bafflement. I felt sure then that she was speaking the truth. She put her hands out flat on the table-cloth like she was having difficulty controlling her feelings.

'What you've just told me is shattering, Mr Faraday.'

'Maybe,' I said. 'I'm afraid you're going to be even more shattered before the evening is over.'

The King number's lower lip quivered. But she only licked her lips with a pink tongue and got up abruptly from the table.

'In that case I'd better serve the dessert before I hear any more. And I'll prepare some strong coffee and liqueurs.'

'You do that,' I said.

I helped her carry the things out to the kitchen and waited while she bustled about preparing the coffee. She handed me the dishes of fruit and cream in silence and I carried them back and sat looking moodily at the haze and the smog and the lights. It was quite dark now but the smog made a sort of fibrous blanket that resembled one of those hazy Impressionist pictures against the lights. It had its own rather terrible beauty.

I got up as the girl's heels rat-tatted over the tiles of the terrace. She put down the tray with the silver coffee pot and went back in for glasses. She didn't speak again until she was opposite and pouring the coffee. I tasted the fruit and cream. Like everything else it was great.

There was something about this girl which reminded me of Stella. It wasn't so much the physical likeness though there were superficial resemblances. Maybe it was her absolute air of integrity. I'd think about it again after I'd seen Stella tomorrow.

The girl passed me the coffee, added sugar to her own.

'A little Armagnac?'

'Fine,' I said.

She filled the miniature glass and pushed it over. Its fierce flavour complemented the strong black coffee perfectly. The girl put her hands together on the table in front of her, the dessert untasted.

'You went out to Mr Vansittart's place, Mr Faraday. He's dead, isn't he? That's what you're trying to tell me?'

'That's it,' I said. 'He was murdered. Someone who knew a good deal about judo killed him with a chop to the neck.'

* * *

The girl drew her breath in with a little implosive noise in the dusk. She made an agitated movement of her hand and her liqueur glass rolled slowly across the table top, the gleaming contents staining the white cloth. I mopped it with my paper napkin, poured her another. She drained it in one gulp, the colour coming back to her cheeks.

'I was the person who found him,' I said. 'That's why I'm not anxious to be tied up with the business just yet. But there was a Japanese gardener out there who may be able to identify me.'

'I don't understand,' the girl said mechanically. 'Why would anyone want to kill him?'

'That's what I intend to find out,' I said. 'And that's why I want your help.'

The girl stared at me, the shock on her face being erased by puzzlement.

'How on earth could I help?'

'You could get that name and address I wanted,' I said. 'From the office files.'

The girl stared at me as though I'd made some outrageous suggestion.

'You don't think it could have had anything to do with his death, Mr Faraday?'

'I don't think anything,' I said. 'I just want the address.'

The girl clasped her slim fingers round the stem of her glass.

'Tonight?'

'Why not?' I said. 'There's no time like the present.'

'I'd like to help,' the girl said, in the same mechanical voice. I guess the impact of my news hadn't worn off yet.

'Let's talk a little more if it's all the same to you.'

'It's all the same to me,' I said. 'Take all the time you want. It must have been a shock.'

'It was, Mr Faraday,' the girl said.

She got up from the table and carried her glass over toward the edge of the balcony. I went across with my coffee cup and stood just behind her. We stayed like that for a few minutes, looking down at the lights and the smog, saying nothing, each of us heavy with our own thoughts.

She turned in the end and stared me in the eye, like she'd come to a decision.

'You want to tell me some more about it, Mr Faraday?'

'Why not,' I said. 'I've gone this far.'

I went back over to the table and re-filled my coffee cup. The girl followed me and stood halfway between the candles and the edge of the balcony, her hands still clasped round the stem of her glass.

'Nothing much to tell, really. Like I told you I said I'd go call on Vansittart. When I got there the front door was open and some Japanese was mowing the lawn. He had a complaint about the mower.'

Karen King smiled faintly.

'That would be Taki,' she said. 'He always had a running war with Giles about his equipment.'

I looked at her closely.

'They got on all right?'

The girl stared at me in turn.

'Sure.'

Her eyes widened.

'You're surely not implying that Taki killed his employer?'

'The thought had occurred to me,' I said. 'He is Japanese. Japanese are good at judo. And the way he was built he could have been responsible for stuffing Vansittart in the bathroom cupboard.'

The girl shook her head, smiling again now.

'You're barking up the wrong tree, Mr Faraday. Unless he's gone stark raving mad, Taki is in the clear. I've known him for some five years and he's a model employee. Sure, he grumbles a lot but Vansittart vouched for his background. He vets all his employees extremely thoroughly. Besides, he comes over to work in the show-rooms sometimes. I'd as soon suspect myself.'

I shrugged.

'If you say so, Miss King. It was just a hunch.'

I felt a small grain of conscience irritating me. About not taking the girl into my entire confidence, of course. But I had enough on my plate at the moment and I didn't know her well enough. The cache of jewellery in my safe was enough to get Vansittart killed ten times over in the right circumstances.

Or the wrong circumstances. All the more reason now for Stella to get the stuff in the bank tomorrow. I'd go over there with her myself first thing. But there was no point in letting the King girl in at this point in time. Though there might be later.

My main priority was to find out where the stuff had come from. For that I had to have the girl on my side. It was obvious she believed my story. Though I had to take into account her shock at my news. For all I knew the whole future of the firm might be in balance, and her financial setup with it. So I didn't press things.

'I'd like to use your phone,' I said.

The interval would give her more time to recover.

'Surely,' she said.

She put her glass down on the table and led the way back through into the living room. She pressed a button and a small ivory telephone came up through the surface of a red leather desk in a corner by the fireplace. It was a neat trick and the girl smiled again at my expression. She looked better now.

'I'll just go freshen up, Mr Faraday.'

I nodded and watched her cross over to one of the far doors which presumably led to a bedroom. I waited until it had closed behind her. I dialled Stella's number. It rang and kept on ringing. I stood there listening to the crackle in the ear-phone, watching the lights of the city through the big windows and thinking what a dumb way I'd chosen to make a living. But then I always say that on every case, whether they're boring or dangerous. There's never a happy mean in my racket.

That reminded me of something else. Tonight I'd break out my Smith-Wesson.38 from the small armoury I keep in a locked cupboard in the bedroom of my rented house over on Park West. It looked like being that sort of case from now on. I listened to the ringing noises. Maybe Stella was in the bath. I put the receiver down and went back on to the balcony. I finished off my coffee and drained the last of the liqueur.

I glanced at my watch. It was still the right side of ten. After a decent interval I went back inside. There was no sign of the girl. I crossed over to the ivory phone and dialled again. There was nothing but the empty ringing tone. I glanced at my watch again. Then I remembered Stella had mentioned earlier in the day that she might take in a new movie tonight. In which case she wouldn't be back much before twelve.

I put the phone back. I debated

whether to look on over at the office. It would be great if someone thought to bust the safe. Though a moment's reflection made me realise that no-one would even know Cramp had had the stuff at this stage. That was why Vansittart had been knocked over. But whoever was after the stuff wouldn't waste much time. I'd get in early to the office and make sure. Or maybe call there on my way home tonight.

I was still standing there when Karen King came back. She wore a lightweight white raincoat and she looked as young and bright as only girls in their twenties can look. She smiled at my expression.

'Let's move, Mr Faraday,' she said. 'The sooner we get you that information the better.'

8

I drove the Buick, with the girl in the passenger seat. She'd wanted to bring her own heap but I thought she might be safer with me. If Vansittart's place was under surveillance as it might well be, Karen King would obviously be a lot better off if she was where I could keep a sharp eye on her. Though I didn't tell her that, of course. She was nervous enough already tonight

The lights were with us and the traffic thin for the time of evening and we made it in good time. I parked two blocks farther down and went around and opened up the passenger door for the girl. I looked sharply up and down the street but I couldn't see anything untoward and there didn't appear to be anyone sitting in the cars parked nearby.

'Have you got a back entrance we can use?' I asked the girl.

Her eyes were wide and questioning again.

'You don't think we're being watched, Mr Faraday?'

I shook my head.

'I don't think anything, but it's best to be on the safe side.'

The girl looked dubious.

'There's the delivery entrance. The main doors are burglar-proof but I have the keys to a small door that's set into it.'

'That's fine,' I said. 'Let's go.'

I followed her down the sidewalk until she turned off into a small, unobtrusive side-alley that bisected the building. Our footsteps echoed unnaturally loudly over the asphalt. The place was just wide enough for a small van and I guessed those would be the only sort of vehicles an outfit like Vansittart's would use for delivery purposes. Anything bigger would use the front. There were lights in armoured glass mountings here, bolted to the brick walls high up and they cast a pallid glare on our faces as we went down.

The girl had her handbag open and I

heard the chinking of keys. We had stopped near the big double doors and now she put the two strangely-shaped keys into a circular lock in a small door set in the right-hand side of the main panel.

'Why all the precautions?' I said. 'I didn't know Vansittart's stock was all that valuable.'

'It isn't in terms of gold, jewellery and cash,' Karen King said. 'But it represents a considerable sum of money from a collecting point of view. Vandals broke in some years ago and did thousands of dollars-worth of damage. That was before my time. But Vansittart swore it would never happen again. So he had all this stuff installed.'

I didn't say anything but the cogs of my mind were revolving again. I waited until the girl had put pressure on the two keys. She opened the door and stepped inside. I went in after her and waited while she locked it behind us. Her hand was on the light-switch when I put mine over hers.

'No lights,' I said. 'Let's just keep this discreet.'

The girl put her mouth up close to my ear. She was trembling slightly.

'I don't quite understand, Mr Faraday.'

I grinned.

'I don't want to attract attention tonight. It's the best way in my business.'

Karen King nodded.

'Just as you say. You'd better keep hold of my hand. I know the way and you'll only be upsetting things otherwise.'

'Just as you say,' I repeated.

There was some light coming through a small window high up and I could have sworn there was a faint flush on her face. Certainly her fingers were trembling as she took my hand. We moved down a dim corridor and I waited again while she put a key into another lock. Like she said, Vansittart had the place well-protected but it seemed excessive to me.

We moved quietly because I'd asked the girl to make our presence as unobtrusive as possible. I couldn't have assigned any valid reason for it but I operated my business mainly on hunches. On more than one occasion I'd stayed alive because of a sixth sense one develops in my line of country.

I just had a feeling about Abel Cramp and his case. Vansittart's death hadn't been a coincidence; I may have been watched coming and going from the girl's place. Without the Smith-Wesson I intended to make my moves as unobtrusively as possible.

'Where would we find the information we're looking for?' I asked the girl.

'Most certainly in Vansittart's office,' the girl breathed, her mouth close to my ear.

She had opened the door now and after negotiating a few glass cases I found we were up at the far end of the vast show-room; the faint light from street-lamps shone in and glistened on the parquet floor and other lights came from neon window fittings and from the cases in the arcade, which were presumably left on all night.

We could see clearly now and Karen King let go my hand. She moved silently down the show-room, the dim lighting gleaming on the glazed eyes and glittering teeth of all the dead animals mounted in the cases and on the shelves. They looked like I felt; baffled and frustrated. We were on a small staircase now and the girl paused.

'How are we going to get in?' I asked.

'The offices are always left open for the cleaners,' the girl whispered. 'All money and confidential information is locked away, of course, in steel safes and filing cabinets.'

She moved quietly on, up the next flight. We were on a large balcony now and the girl led the way on thick carpeting toward a door at the right. The dim lighting in here gleamed on gold lettering: Managing Director. Private.

The girl had the door open. She went in in front of me. I heard a faint scuffle in the blackness. The office was in darkness. I guess the drapes were drawn. I had my hand out for the light-switch when something hit me on the back of the neck and I went out in a brilliant display of Roman candles.

★ ★ ★

My mouth tasted of blood and stale peanut shucks. I rolled over, felt my fingers touch something hard. I listened to a groaning noise, realised it was myself. I got hold of the hard surface, found it was the leg of a desk or table. I hauled myself upright, stopped when I felt shooting pains at the back of my neck. There was a faint light from the landing coming in the half-open door. I found the light-switch, buttoned it.

I had to close my eyes because the light was too bright. I opened them again, took in the state of the office. Drawers were open, the door of a cupboard sagged on its hinges and there was a sea of papers lapping round the legs of the big mahogany desk that had belonged to Vansittart. The pyjama-suited legs of Karen King were protruding from beyond the desk.

I got round there quick. She was breathing heavily. I smelt the sickly hospital smell of chloroform then. There was a faint burning round her mouth. It was obvious someone had held a chloroform pad over her mouth and nose.

That was the faint noise I had heard before I'd been sapped. I went over and pulled the drapes, opened the steel-framed window to clear the atmosphere.

Then I sat down again, feeling the base of my neck. Someone had chopped me there with tremendous force. I was lucky my spine was still in one piece. I'd have a headache and bruising for a day or two but otherwise I couldn't find any other damage. I sat there for perhaps ten minutes before I took any real interest in the scene.

Then I went over and picked up Karen King. She was pretty heavy for such a slim girl and I was bushed before I'd got her comfortable on a leather divan at one side of the office. I went out in rear and found Vansittart's private washroom. I made a pad of a clean towel I found there and wet it. I went back to the girl, sprinkled water on her face and put the pad on her forehead.

She was breathing comfortably and her complexion was back to normal now. Then I sat down again and lit a cigarette. I surveyed the office while I smoked, assessing the situation. The window at the far side had been smashed; that was presumably where the intruder had got in. When I felt up to it I opened the casement and looked out. There was a flat roof just below. Fragments of glass glinted dully in the light of the street-lamps. Whoever had been after Vansittart's records could have been halfway to San Francisco by now.

I looked at my watch. As far as I could gather I'd been out for more than half an hour. It had been some blow. I eased my neck with the fingers of my right hand, the pain slowly subsiding. Then I went back into the centre of the office and gave my attention to the files. Whoever had been in here hadn't had time to complete the job.

There was a block of grey steel filing cabinets at one side; there was a typed card in the slot at the top which said: CONFIDENTIAL. An attempt had been made to open the drawers; the metal was all gashed and incised like a blunt knife or maybe a cold chisel had been used. I tried the drawers. All of them were still securely locked. I wished then I'd gone through Vansittart's effects more thoroughly. Maybe I'd have found his keys.

That raised another question. Why hadn't the killer taken them from his house. Because I'd maybe turned up too soon? Like now? It was possible. The more I thought about it the more I came to the conclusion that it was amateur work. I heard a little moaning noise then. The girl was coming around. I went over to the office door, closed it and locked it from the inside. I didn't intend to be surprised again tonight.

I stood looking down at the girl. She had her eyes open now. Then she was wide awake, alarm on her face. I pressed her back on the divan as she tried to get up.

'Take it easy,' I said. 'Just lie there for a bit.'

'What happened?' Karen King said.

'Someone was here,' I said. 'He chloroformed you and knocked me out. A pretty hefty customer.'

I could still feel the shooting pains through my skull. Karen King had a disbelieving look on her face as she took in the information.

'This whole thing is crazy,' she said. 'What would anyone want in Vansittart's files?'

I shrugged.

'That address we're looking for for starters.'

The girl was up now. She swayed on the divan and I put my hand on her shoulder to steady her.

'But why?'

'There's a lot of money involved,' I said. 'That's all I can tell you for the moment.'

The girl was on her feet. She came close to me and looked up into my face.

'You think it was the same person or persons who killed Vansittart?'

'Looks like it,' I said. 'It means the police will be here tomorrow. I shouldn't touch anything. Leave it to the cleaners to find.'

I looked round the wreckage of the office thoughtfully.

'We'd better get our story straight,' I said. 'I don't want you to tell any lies but

I'd appreciate you keeping my name out of it. It would be too complicated otherwise. Apart from cramping my style.'

'Certainly, Mr Faraday,' Karen King said. 'I don't think that will be too difficult. But I wish I knew why.'

'You and me both,' I said.

I flicked the ash off my cigarette into the pack, crushed out the butt and put that back too. The girl stood and watched me gravely. I went around the room once or twice and then came back to her.

'How well do you know Vansittart's operation?'

'Inside out,' the girl said. 'If you mean business; the technical side and so on. If you're asking about his customers I don't know them all.'

I looked over toward the file cabinets.

'How did you intend to get into those?'

The girl smiled faintly. She walked over toward them and I followed.

'There's no secret if you know the system. I have a duplicate set of keys. Mr Vansittart had a set of mine. It was necessary, in case of accident or one of us being taken ill. The combined files give a complete record of the work on hand for individuals and institutions.'

'What I'm looking for is confidential stuff,' I said. 'Big customers; probably an individual, not an institution. Material received within the past few days.'

The girl stared at me, bewilderment in her eyes.

'I don't really know what you're driving at, Mr Faraday. But there shouldn't be any problem. Vansittart put that sort of stuff in what he called his Z file.'

She moved down the end of the cabinet, her keys out again.

'You're sure you're all right,' I said.

She nodded.

'I'm fine, now. Just delayed shock.'

She opened up the drawer and took out several dockets.

'Just three cards which might interest you, Mr Faraday.'

Her mouth was set in a grim line beneath the dim light of the overhead lamp.

'I see what you meant about prohibited stuff. I find this indefensible.'

'You're talking about a couple of

mountain eagles,' I said.

The girl nodded. She handed me a large piece of pasteboard from the file.

'Seems I didn't know Mr Vansittart at all.'

'The tip of the iceberg,' I said. 'So we've both got something to hide now.'

Little sparks of anger were dancing in Karen King's eyes.

'If I'm to carry on this business all this sort of thing is going to stop.'

'Take it easy,' I said. 'Now you know why I was being discreet. You wouldn't like this business to get out. I'd rather not tell you my client's name or the basis of my inquiries. We help one another.'

The girl nodded, her blonde hair falling round her face in a cloud of beaten gold.

'Life is complicated, Mr Faraday.'

'And death,' I said. 'I find that in my racket all the time.'

I glanced at the card, gave a low whistle.

'Hugo Merrick,' I said. 'The millionaire sportsman?'

The girl inclined her head.

'That's the one. Vansittart handled all

his stuff personally.'

'I bet he did,' I said.

I took the card back to the desk and copied out the address. There was a telephone number, marked exdirectory, and I took that down too. Then I gave the details back to the girl and watched while she re-locked them in the file.

'Who else has sets of keys for these,' I said.

'No-one, Mr Faraday. Just Mr Vansittart and myself.'

'I was just wondering why the killer didn't take Vansittart's own set,' I said. 'Probably because I was too closely on his track.'

The girl shivered suddenly like she was cold.

'What do you know about Van Horn?' I said.

Karen King looked startled.

'Curator of the Museum of Ornithology? Nothing, other than that he's highly respected in ornithological circles.'

She stared at me for a long moment.

'Do you mean, is he straight?'

There was a blank silence between us.

'Who knows after this?' the girl said with a helpless little shrug.

She went over to sit on the divan again.

'You're tired,' I said. 'And you've had two bad scenes in one evening. I'll take you home.'

I smiled down at her.

'On the way we'll rehearse what you're going to say to the police in the morning.'

9

'Well, well, Mike,' Stella said. 'So we got a big one.'

'Looks like it,' I said.

We'd just returned from the bank and now I sat at my old broadtop and studied Merrick's address again. It was a place called El Capitan set atop a bluff up in the hills some miles out of town. I knew where because I'd been up there on another case some years before. It was an estate running to about two hundred acres and from what I'd heard would be difficult to get into. Doubly difficult in view of my present errand.

Stella looked at the big headlines on page 3 of The Examiner again. I guessed Vansittart would have been annoyed not to have made the front if he'd known about it. He sounded like that sort of character. It was hotter than ever this morning and I'd taken my jacket off and draped it across the back of my swivel chair.

'This girl Karen King sounds rather nice, Mike,' Stella said vaguely.

She looked at me from under lowered lids as she went over her shorthand notes again. I grinned. I wasn't going to be drawn on that one this morning. Stella glanced at her wrist-watch and crossed her legs with a little caressing sound that always sent my blood-count up.

'Abel Cramp was on the wire just before you came in, Mike. I thought he was going to have a heart attack.'

'Too much to hope for,' I said.

Stella shot me a quick glance. There was ninety per cent reproach in it, so I changed my tack.

'What did you tell him?'

'The usual bromide,' Stella said. 'That you were making progress.'

She got up from the desk.

'You want coffee now? You'll need it if you're going out to Merrick's place.'

'Who said I was?' I asked, looking at the sun-dazzle at the window blinds.

Stella paused by my desk.

'Well, aren't you?'

I grinned.

'Maybe. It'll be cooler in the mountains anyway.'

Stella went over to the alcove and I heard the snick of the coffee percolator going on.

'Cramp's not to know those birds came from Merrick,' I said.

'Of course not,' Stella said. 'That goes without saying.'

There was reproach in her voice now. I should have known better but I was a little edgy this morning. I swivelled in my chair, the bulk of the Smith-Wesson comforting against my chest muscles in its nylon harness. I looked at the image of Stella's golden hair against the frosted glass. The pain had gone from my head now but I could still feel it when I moved too suddenly.

'That character who downed you must have had some nerve, Mike,' Stella said. 'To fix the girl before he turned to you. And you didn't see anything.'

'It's happened before,' I said. 'But I'm inclined to agree with you.'

116

Stella came back and sat on the edge of my desk, swinging a shapely knee. It was a little disconcerting this morning and I swivelled my chair in the opposite direction. Stella's blue eyes were very thoughtful as she caught the movement. She slid off the desk and went back to the alcove. I sat, my eyes closed, inhaling the rich aroma of the roasted beans.

I sensed the shadow of her body passing between me and the window and opened my eyes in time to see her putting my cup down. She went back for her own, pushed the biscuit tin over. I sat stirring my coffee and looking at her as she sat in the client's chair at the opposite side of my desk.

'You were lucky, Mike,' she said.

I shrugged.

'Whoever hit me didn't mean to kill me.'

Stella shook her head, the sun glinting on the gold bell of her hair.

'I didn't mean that. I'm talking about the Japanese gardener. Taki, wasn't it? He gave a pretty good description of you. But one which might fit a hundred thousand other men in the L.A. basin.'

'There is that,' I said. 'More importantly, he didn't notice my heap or get the number.'

'But they still got a print of your golf-soles in the wet patch around the bath,' Stella said.

I winced. Despite my care I'd overlooked that.

'I changed my shoes this morning,' I said.

Stella smiled.

'Master-mind,' she said. 'My God, Mike, if you'd turned that brain of yours to crime the police wouldn't stand a chance.'

I didn't bother to top that. But Stella's amusement lasted her until I left to tool on out to the El Capitan estate.

* * *

I stopped for lunch on the way and it was early afternoon when I got there. Like always I hadn't any real plan of campaign and I just meant to keep digging around to see what I'd come up with. Like I figured it was cooler in the hills and the wind on the exposed edges of the canyons was so strong I put my jacket on again. I reviewed the case again for perhaps the thirtieth time since I started.

Not that it did any good. But it was supposed to be therapeutic for the brain. The Parker woman had given her deposition to the police. She hadn't seen the Japanese and the Japanese hadn't seen her. But she'd played the bell in the porch for a while, raised no-one and gone back home somewhat out of temper with Vansittart I'd gathered. It was about what I'd figured.

I'd been lucky with the old dame with the shears too. She could have sworn I'd come out in a Ford Thunderbird. And she'd described me as a man in his early sixties with a goatee beard. My fit of chuckling had lasted me all the way into town this morning. I couldn't have had two better witnesses from my point of view. Except that they'd have been equally unhelpful from the point of view of identifying the killer.

I stuck to my previous guess. He'd

obviously come in across the back of the garden and slipped in while the gardener was otherwise engaged. Obviously, just before my arrival and that of the Parker woman. But it had been nicely timed. He'd then waited until after dark before trying Vansittart's office. I'd been out of luck both times.

I reviewed what I knew about Hugo Merrick. Which wasn't much. He was a man of about forty, married three times already, of course; divorced three times. Like most extremely wealthy men he kept a low profile. He was keen on polo, shooting and deep-sea fishing and from what I could make out from Karen King and Vansittart's files, regularly sent specimens to be mounted up.

So far as I knew he kept them on his estate at El Capitan and he had also founded a natural history museum in his native city of San Francisco. Stella had dug up most of that information this morning, with her usual efficiency. My knowledge of natural history and ornithology was practically nil, as Karen King had guessed. I couldn't hope to fool a man like Merrick. Once again I had to play it by ear. But I'd think of something. I could have phoned Merrick's estate, of course. I didn't even know if he was there. But I had another of my hunches about him. And I've found that people often find it easier to deal with a person on the spot when they sometimes give things away.

It's too easy to fend people off at the other end of a phone. That was my theory anyway, and I was stuck with it. I looked at my large-scale on the dash-board in front of me and turned off at the next intersection, the minor road snaking up into the foothills where ridges of shimmering blue were painted a pale lemon-yellow by the sunlight on the upper branches of the trees.

El Capitan estate on El Capitan bluff was as unobtrusive as a millionaire's estate can be. And that means pretty unobtrusive nowadays, what with assassinations, kidnappings and political threats. I hunted back and forth for more than a quarter of an hour before I spotted the sunken lane, carefully disguised with flowering shrubs, high hedges and over-hanging trees.

I turned the Buick off the main stem and on to a narrow triangular section of tarmac which had an overgrown area of grass in the middle. Only when I had the Buick's bonnet lined up on the lane did I see the small white finger-post which spelled out in black Gothic lettering: El Capitan.

I bumped on down in low gear, the high flowering hedges coming in so close they seemed to block out the sky. I went on this way for more than half a mile, noting the hacked-out laybys every few hundred yards. Otherwise, there would have been no possible chance of passing in such a confined space.

I wondered just what it was about Hugo Merrick that called for all this security. It was obvious that the terrain, the width of the lane, even the surface, which had large humps in it every so often had been designed with one specific purpose; to reduce the speed of the visitor's vehicle to an idling crawl.

I got out into the sunlight at the other

end. I was in an oval of tarmac and beyond, the driveway went on, only this time it was much wider and planted with an imposing avenue of mature poplars. For a moment it looked like one of those colour prints of Versailles that the L.A. travel agents sport in their windows every spring. And there wasn't a sign of the house yet.

I stopped the Buick then, wound down the passenger window to let some more of the fresh air through, and set fire to a cigarette. The bird song was deafening up here. I sat thinking about nothing for a couple of minutes, putting the spent match-stalk in the dashboard tray mechanically, closing the drawer afterward, without even being conscious of the movement.

It was then I noticed the security lights. They were strung out among the trees on heavy duty cables, their armoured glass casings screwed to posts set next the trees and fairly high up among the branches. That wasn't all Merrick had got going for him either. There was another big post set up in the middle of the concourse on which I was parked. That had a frosted glass lantern set atop it.

I was inclined to dismiss it at its face value at first but as I glanced at it for the second time I saw that I'd missed out on something. It was slowly revolving on its axis. I spotted it for what it was then. Unless I missed my guess it was a hidden TV camera, shooting from behind some sort of opaque ambulance type glass, monitoring my movements. This was getting interesting. I resisted an impulse to make a rude gesture toward it and smoked on as though I was unaware and unconcerned.

But it was obvious that my arrival had been noted by Merrick's people a mile or more before I got to his estate entrance. Which posed some extremely interesting questions. If all this elaboration were carried to its logical conclusion they may have been alerted to my presence as soon as I got off the main road. Probably by a cable hidden under the tarmac at the lane entrance which would have activated alarm bells or flashing lights up at the house. Or most likely, at the lodge.

I finished my cigarette with a great show of outward unconcern. Then I pitched it out the window where it sputtered and expired on the tarmac. The lantern atop the post had been stationary all the while but as I re-started the Buick's motor and idled past it commenced its stealthy circling again. Probably I was making as good a close-up as Cary Grant ever registered on someone's monitor screen right now.

I put the Buick's snout at the entrance of the avenue of poplars and glided slowly up. The trees seemed to loom down over the road like they were waiting to engorge me.

10

The avenue went straight for another half-mile and then took a gentle curve to the left. I followed it mechanically, not bothering how many security devices there might be. The sunlight made a dazzling stipple of bough-patterns on my face and even the freshness of the air beneath the welcome shade of the trees did little to dispel the lassitude that was creeping over me. One always gets it when driving in the heat and today was no exception.

I passed a big white board up near the end of the avenue which said: EL CAPITAN ESTATE. Strictly Private, but I kept on going. I hadn't come this far to be put off by notice boards. I still hadn't got my story straight but my dialogue would come all right once I got to grips with somebody human. All these wide open spaces and electronic devices didn't give the unprepared visitor much of a

126

chance. Which was no doubt the object of the exercise.

I passed the curve in the drive and came up another big concourse which looked more like something out of a zoo-park than anything to be found on a private estate. For starters there was a large stretch of water sparkling in the sunshine. It was a man-made canal which ran arrow-straight at this point from the woods on either side the road. The banks were very steep; in fact they weren't banks at all but walls of dressed stone which leaned outward so that anyone in the water wouldn't be able to climb out. He would either drown or have to try downstream somewhere. The canal was about thirty feet across and the brownish water was in a constant state of agitation by the action of the wind.

There was a metal bridge spanning the canal which led to a metal entrance gate, with a white-painted lodge inside the wire-mesh fencing that flanked the far bank of the canal. What was interesting was that the bridge didn't come all the way over. There was about ten feet between its edge and the shore on my side. I drew the Buick up carefully and killed the motor. I noticed there was a heavy steel plate let into the concrete at the edge of the canal.

It was evident from the heavy friction marks on the plate that the bridge was operated by hydraulic machinery housed in a sort of concrete island in the middle of the canal and on which the centre span of the bridge was balanced. I got out the Buick and stretched myself. The sun shone blandly on the windows of the lodge but there was no-one in sight and I might have been the only person in the world.

There was a grey metal box atop a post at the edge of the canal and I strolled over toward it. When I was about three yards off a red light glowed and a voice, heavy and suspicious, growled from the speaker.

'Your name?'

'Faraday,' I said.

'Your business, Mr Faraday?'

'I'd like to see Mr Merrick,' I said.

The voice was polite but even the speaker grille seemed to exude suspicion.

'Have you an appointment?'

I shrugged.

'No. I didn't know one was necessary.'

'Mr Merrick is a busy man,' the speaker said. 'He doesn't see anyone without an appointment.'

'I think he'd see me if he knew what I'd come about,' I said.

'What is your business?' the speaker said.

'You're repeating yourself,' I said.

There was a moment of angry silence. Evidently I'd said the wrong thing.

'I'm still asking, Mr Faraday.'

'It's private,' I said.

'I very much regret we can't take things any further,' the voice said. 'Looks like you've had your trip for nothing.'

'Maybe,' I said. 'Is there anyone else I could see? Someone from Mr Merrick's estate? His secretary? Or a senior member of his staff.'

There was another moody silence.

'Where you from, Mr Faraday?'

'L.A.', I said. 'It's a long way.'

'No-one asked you to come,' the voice said.

'This is beginning to sound like something out of Two Thousand and One,' I said.

The speaker didn't bother to answer that.

'We don't encourage visitors, Mr Faraday. But I'll find out what I can. It may take a quarter of an hour.'

'I'll hang on,' I said. 'I've got all the time in the world.'

I went back over to the Buick. There was a click in the speaker grille and the static cut out. A dead silence crawled back in, broken only by the distant song of birds and the faint lapping of water in the canal as it flowed between its stone walls. I left both front doors of the Buick open and lit another cigarette.

The sun shone brilliantly down on the white innocence of the lodge; on the steel slats of the bridge; on the private road which ran white and arrow-straight back from the far shore; and on the restless wavelets of the canal. I sat there for what seemed like a year. Then the speaker crackled again. I got out the car and went

130

on over, my shadow dark and heavy in the hot dust.

★　★　★

'You're in luck, Mr Faraday,' the speaker said. 'Miss Fallowfield will see you.'

'Who might she be?' I said.

'Mr Merrick's secretary. She handles all his confidential matters. If she passes you, you get to see Mr Merrick. If not, you don't.'

'Fine,' I said. 'Seems I'm in luck.'

'That remains to be seen,' the speaker said enigmatically. 'You may find it easier to get in than out if you're not on the up and up.'

'I'm on the up,' I said.

I turned back to the Buick but the voice in the speaker was peremptory now.

'Leave your heap there.'

I shrugged. I walked over, closed the doors and got the keys. I walked back toward the edge of the canal. There was a faint whining noise now. The end of the bridge was coming slowly toward me, cantilevered out from the central island. I jumped aboard just before it reached the shore and walked down over its echoing surface toward the far bank. I could feel the steel plates quivering beneath me and looking over my shoulder saw that the decking was drawing away from the shore again. Already the Buick looked infinitely small and remote.

As I stepped on the opposite bank a tall, lean young man with blond, crew-cut hair came out the lodge gates. He was carrying a shotgun casually under one arm and he walked with loose, athletic strides toward the big gates. He put his hand against them and they rumbled aside automatically. He wore blue jeans and a red and black check shirt but his eyes were ice-blue and his face hard and venal.

'You got any identification, Mr Faraday?'

He stopped about two yards from me, the gate just between us but I noticed the barrel of his gun was levelled at my gut.

'Driver's licence do?' I said.

'Sure.'

I fished in my wallet and handed it to

him. He studied it in silence and threw it back.

'Why all the Castle Dracula stuff?' I said.

He shrugged.

'If you had as much money and responsibilities as Mr Merrick I guess you'd take a few precautions too.'

'Maybe,' I said.

We were walking through the gate now. I heard a sudden bleeping noise. The blond man's face was hard and suspicious again. He brought the barrel of the shotgun up, white showing round his nostrils.

'The piece, Mr Faraday. If you please. And take it easy.'

I reached in my holster and took out the Smith-Wesson. I broke it and emptied the shells into my hand. I gave them to him, put the gun back in my holster.

'That satisfy you?' I said.

He looked at me angrily and then down at the shells in his palm.

'I guess so,' he said. 'Why do you carry it?'

'Why do you carry the shotgun?' I said.

'Because Southern California's a violent place.'

He grinned suddenly.

'All right, Mr Faraday. I'll buy it. I've taken quite a shine to you already.'

'That's something to be thankful for,' I said.

I stared up the shimmering distances of the avenue.

'What do we do now? Walk?'

The blond man shook his head. He grinned again.

'Transport is all laid on, Mr Faraday.'

He led the way up toward the lodge, the gates whining to behind us. His voice wasn't the same as the one on the speaker so I guessed there was at least one other man in the lodge. These people were maintaining high security up here and I didn't aim to give them any excuses for a fatal accident. I was a long way from L.A. now. Millionaires were sometimes eccentric, sure; but I guessed Merrick had a lot more to hide than a few illegally shot game-birds. I grinned to myself at the thought.

The blond man looked at me sidewise.

'Private or official cop, Mr Faraday?'

I looked at him blandly.

'Nothing like that.'

He shook his head, a pained expression on his face.

'Come off it, Mr Faraday. You got private dick written all over you.'

'I didn't know it showed,' I said.

He licked his lips and led the way around the side of the stone lodge.

'We wouldn't be letting you up if we didn't think we could trust you, Mr Faraday. We don't mind private dicks. Or official ones come to that. Mr Merrick's got nothing to hide.'

'Glad to hear it,' I said.

The blond character shook his head irritably.

'What Mr Merrick doesn't like are reporters from scandal sheets and dirt-digging newspapers. Photographers and such-like. He's had some bad scenes with them over the past years.'

'Sorry about that,' I said.

Either the blond man had a thick skin or he was taking my words at their face value. He led me up a small entry leading off the main drive. There was a sort of enlarged version of an electric golf buggy sitting there. It had a big sun-shade on it, was painted yellow and had the letters 14 in big figures in black paint on the side.

The blond guard slid behind the wheel, putting the shotgun barrel first into a leather holster at the side of the contraption. I got up next him in the passenger seat.

'I'm too young to die like this,' I said.

'You got a great sense of humour, Mr Faraday,' he said between his teeth.

We whined smoothly up the aching white distances of the road.

11

'You got a name?' I said.

The blond character looked at me.

'For why?'

I shrugged.

'Just curiosity.'

The blond man smiled a dead smile, revealing square yellow teeth.

'No reason you shouldn't know. Bo Henderson.'

'You worked for Merrick long?' I said.

Henderson shook his head.

'That's restricted information, Mr Faraday. Ask me something else.'

I glanced at him sharply. He was acting like we were on a TV quiz programme.

'All right,' I said. 'Who's this secretary I'm going to see?'

He grinned. There was genuine humour on his face now. He turned the electric buggy round the far turn of the drive. There was a sort of landscaped mound on the right-hand side with something that looked like a Chinese pagoda on the top of it. It had a green pantile roof and as we mounted a steep side-road that led to it a stone terrace with white-painted tables gleaming in the sunlight started coming up.

'Miss Fallowfield? Susan Fallowfield. You're a lucky man, Mr Faraday.'

'How do you make that out?' I said.

Henderson frowned, concentrating on the steering as we ascended the steep curves. Alternate bars of sunlight and shadow fell across his hard, sunburned face.

'Firstly, she hardly ever sees any visitors. Secondly, she's quite a looker. She's the only one can do anything with Merrick.'

He gave me a sidewise look.

'Don't take that the wrong way, Mr Faraday. I don't know what she gets up to with Merrick in private. There was some talk around the estate. Not that it's any of my business. But it's strange, the hold she has over him.'

He skilfully shaved by the edge of an overhanging boulder as we mounted into full sunlight again.

'Dames,' he said. 'They got it all ways. Now, I've done some useful work around here. But I can't get anywhere. I'm stuck down at the gate. Can't get any more money either.'

'Why do you stay, then?' I said.

Henderson gave me another sidewise look.

'Good question, Mr Faraday. Steady, undemanding work with plenty of off-time. And there are one or two fringe benefits.'

He chuckled deep in his throat.

'Don't think I'm grumbling, really. It's just that we don't often have a chance to talk with strangers. Merrick likes everyone to stay close. So we have a lot of entertainment facilities within the estate.'

'Like what?' I said.

'Swim-pools, shooting-ranges. The opportunity to indulge in private tastes and hobbies.'

'Sounds fine,' I said.

The blond man shook his head again.

'You want to try it up here for a year or two, Mr Faraday. You get a little stir-crazy.'

We were almost up to the pagoda by now.

'This where Merrick lives?' I said.

Henderson looked at me increduously.

'Hell no, Mr Faraday. This is just the guest-house. Where Mr Merrick's private visitors stay. Miss Fallowfield meets people like you down here. It's more convenient, you see. And ensures Mr Merrick's privacy.'

I looked down at the toes of my brogues. Like always, they were scuffed.

'What did you mean just now. About the girl?'

Henderson took his eye off the drive which had stopped snaking around now and was flattening and broadening out in front of us between the banks of thick rhododendron and tropical foliage. There was a cloying scent in the air.

'You said something about the hold she had over him.'

Henderson took one hand off the wheel and scratched the roots of his hair reflectively.

'Merrick's a man used to being around women, Mr Faraday. As you probably

know, he's been married two, three times.
You know how these rich guys are.'

'I don't,' I said. 'You tell me.'

Henderson nodded approvingly, like he
was glad I didn't mix with the wealthy
set.

'Before Miss Fallowfield came Merrick
was the most ruthless guy you ever saw.
After she came he changed.'

'For the better?' I said.

He shrugged.

'Depends which side of the fence
you're on. The girl seems to give the
orders now. We hardly ever see Merrick in
person. Swings and roundabouts. Where
Merrick would be hard with some of the
estate people, she's soft. And vice versa. It
can vary from day to day.'

'Could be awkward,' I said.

Henderson turned the steering wheel
with a flourish.

'You can say that again.'

He saved me the trouble because we'd
arrived by now and he drew up the buggy
with a flourish at the bottom of a big
flight of steps.

'This is as far as we go, Mr Faraday.

You're on your own from here on in. Miss Fallowfield may be up there or not. If she isn't just wait on the terrace. Don't go fooling around in the grounds.'

I caught his angry eyes with my own.

'I won't,' I said.

He nodded frostily.

'When Miss Fallowfield's finished with you give her time to get back to the house. You'll find an ivory telephone on one of the tables. It's got several buttons on the base. Press the one marked Gate. I'll come up and fetch you back.'

'Much obliged,' I said.

I got down from the buggy and watched him turn round with skilful, trained movements of the controls.

'That's what I'm paid for,' he said.

I watched him whine back down among the banks of thick rhododendron. Then I turned to the steps and started climbing.

* * *

The terrace was empty when I got there. It sat under the burning sun in an ocean of greenness; with the jade-green of the heavy tiled roofs of the guest-house and with the massive banks of greenery and rhododendron all about I might have been somewhere in Burma. I stood there for a moment or two, wondering whether the Fallowfield number might be waiting in the house, but she didn't show.

I lit a cigarette and went over toward the big French doors which punctuated the elegant classical façade. They were all securely locked and I moved slowly down the terrace, admiring the decor and killing time. I saw the telephone Henderson had mentioned on one of the white tables scattered about and as I turned to sit down I saw what I should have noticed all along if I hadn't had my back to it when I was climbing the steps.

It looked like a cross between the Taj Mahal; the Prince Regent's Brighton Pavilion; and Louis' place at Versailles. Layer after layer of brilliant cake-icing glittered in the hard sun, the light from the windows in the wing which faced the terrace the other side of the valley giving back thousands of reflections.

There was a lot more of it, but I've given the general impression. The Taj Mahal would have seemed like a Monogram film set by comparison. There were cupolas and towers and turrets in classical pantiling; and even gilded and copper domes. It should have looked like Disneyland but somehow solid architectural skill and a basic grounding in taste saved it.

The place was set on a sort of plateau raised up from the deer-park which faced me; a big lake fringed by trees glittered in the sun and deer were grazing peaceably in the middle distance. A white automobile was gliding along the frontage of Merrick's mansion on a deep-set driveway which must have been set back behind the terrace. The place was so big it seemed to take it about five minutes to get clear of the building.

There were fountains on the terrace too and massive, eighteenth century style staircases with heavy balustrades and ornamental vases of flowers on the connecting pillars zig-zagged down from the mound into the park below. I didn't know which was designed for which. The guest-house for the guests to admire the mansion; or the mansion so Merrick could keep an eye on the guests. A little bit of both, perhaps.

I was glad I hadn't been invited to meet Miss Fallowfield at the main house. I would only have gotten lost and probably starved to death long before I'd found her. I sat back on the terrace, admiring the view and smoking, for perhaps ten minutes. There was no sound except the faint echo of bird-song and the almost imperceptible rustle of branches. I guessed this was maybe the Fallowfield number's way of softening up the visitors.

Certainly I'd ceased beating my brains out over Cramp's problems and my own; even Stella and L.A. seemed far away. Not geographically, but somewhere in time and atmosphere. That was the sort of effect the place had on you.

There was a brilliant flash on the horizon now. The white car had finished its sedate drift along the terrace and had turned down another white road, drawn as straight as a line on graph paper, which obviously met the private lane up which I'd travelled with Henderson. I could see it was a Rolls now and the sun was striking sparks from the windshield, the silver lady and the radiator grille.

I admired its progress all the way down. I thought for a moment that maybe ex-President Nixon had been paying a visit but dismissed it. More likely that Merrick himself was setting out on one of his anonymous visits to board his private yacht somewhere along the coast. I was surprised he hadn't built his own canal through to link up with the Pacific. Hearst would have liked him if he'd still been around. They had something of the same style.

I finished my cigarette and stubbed it out in a metal tray on the slatted table in front of me. If it was Merrick there was nothing I could do about it. I guess I was lucky to be able to see the girl. I could possibly read something from the necessarily guarded conversation which would ensue. The Rolls disappeared from view beneath a thick belt of trees and the spectacle was over.

I got up from my seat and walked over

to the edge of the terrace. The view was even better here and I could see down into the deep bowl of green that the park made at this point. A tall, slim girl with dark hair was making her way unhurriedly across the small valley that separated us. She was obviously at home there and the deer were evidently used to her for they went on contentedly browsing, taking no notice as she walked among them.

She had certainly come down one of the sets of steps opposite and she knew I'd arrived because she shaded her eyes to look up toward the guest house from time to time. I thought about going down to meet her but remembered what Henderson had said and stayed where I was. The girl was closer now. She was walking with rangy, athletic strides. She wore tan slacks and a blue shirt and even though a considerable distance separated us I could see what Henderson meant.

She was worth looking at. I stood there at the edge of the terrace, the sun warm on my cheek, a faint breeze cooling the surroundings, and waited for her to climb up to meet me.

12

The girl gave me a dazzling smile as she came up the last few yards of the steps. She held out a small, brown hand, slightly breathless after the steep climb from the park.

'Sorry to keep you waiting, Mr Faraday. Welcome to Camelot.'

I grinned. Susan Fallowfield looked at me appraisingly from frank brown eyes.

'The visitors always say that, Mr Faraday. So I like to get in first.'

'You did, Miss Fallowfield,' I said.

The girl walked quickly over toward the nearest table. It had a green and white striped umbrella and was in thick shade anyway,

'I think we'll be comfortable here,' she said, sitting down with the lithe movements that characterised everything she did.

'It was good of you to see me at all,' I said.

The girl turned down the corners of her mouth which gave her an expression made familiar by scores of Bette Davis movies. Then she smiled, though still with a wryness lurking at the corners of her mouth.

'I always find it's better to meet problems head on.'

I looked at her in surprise.

'You think I pose a problem, Miss Fallowfield?'

'I haven't made up my mind yet, Mr Faraday.'

I got out my pack of cigarettes and offered her one. She took it with small, pink-nailed fingers and puffed nervously as I lit it for her. That reminded me of Bette Davis too.

'You're frank at any rate,' I said.

She shrugged.

'We shall have to see whether you'll be equally frank in return.'

I shifted on my teak-slatted seat, looking out over toward the white wedding cake that was Merrick's mansion.

'I'll try,' I said.

The girl was entirely different from what I'd expected. Not that she was unassuming. Far from it. Henderson was a hundred per cent on the button there all right. Her glistening dark hair was cut in Louise Brooks fashion, with the edges curving away from her ears. She wore diamond earrings that must have cost a small fortune. For a moment I wished Stella had been present to give me an appraisal.

Her face was full, her cheeks well-rounded; she had good bone structure and her chin was firm and purposeful. Henderson's words went through my mind as I studied her through filmy clouds of tobacco smoke. Her skin was healthy and lightly tanned and as she opened her mouth to remove the cigarette, I could see she had even, flawless teeth. She removed a speck of tobacco from her full lower lip with the tip of a pink tongue.

She had long, natural eye-lashes and her make-up, unobtrusively applied, merely enhanced a natural attractiveness that was already there. For the rest she had a good body; firm, full breasts; a flat stomach and long, well-shaped legs that the thin material of her trousers did little to hide. She must have known what I was thinking because her eyes suddenly became clouded, perhaps with annoyance or irritation. It was difficult to tell.

'I can give you an hour, Mr Faraday,' she said, looking at a gold and platinum wristlet watch that must have cost a good deal too.

'Not a minute longer.'

I smiled.

'It won't take anywhere that long, Miss Fallowfield.'

She nodded, sitting upright in the chair and becoming suddenly alert.

'Why do you carry a gun, Mr Faraday?'

'So Henderson told you?' I said.

She shrugged.

'Of course. That's what he's there for. To vet people and let the house know. You haven't answered my question.'

'It's part of my business,' I said. 'I'm a private detective.'

I knew if Henderson had told her about the Smith-Wesson he would probably have voiced other suspicions, so I had nothing to lose by putting a major card down. For all I knew Henderson, or the other man in the lodge, might have already come to that conclusion by using their TV cameras, before I even arrived at the Camelot drawbridge. And it might have been one of the major factors influencing the girl to see me.

She nodded her head slowly, like I'd said the right thing.

'That's what the man at the gate thought,' she said. 'You mind showing me your identification?'

'Not at all.'

I passed over the photostat to her. She studied it carefully, a stray beam of sunlight making a little streak of fire across the calm beauty of her face. She handed it back in silence, her eyes searching my face.

'Now what would a private detective want up here with a man like Mr Merrick?' she said.

I shifted again in my chair.

'A good question,' I said. 'And one it's a little difficult in getting around to.'

The girl glanced at her watch again. It could have become an irritating habit.

'We have precisely fifty-three minutes, Mr Faraday.'

'The time is immaterial, Miss Fallowfield,' I said. 'What I have to say won't take long.'

The girl flushed and threw her dark hair back from her face with an impatient gesture.

'I wish you'd get to it then, Mr Faraday.'

'I will,' I promised her. 'But you may not like it.'

* * *

A heavy silence descended between us. The girl crossed her slim legs in the tan slacks and stared at me with little sparks of anger in her eyes.

'I don't think I quite understand, Mr Faraday. You'll have to spell it out for me.'

I nodded.

'Fair enough.'

I decided to give her both barrels. We'd been sparring round long enough.

'Mr Merrick is an internationally-known sportsman, I believe. A man who's interested in natural history and ornithology as well.'

The girl nodded distantly.

'These are well-established facts, Mr Faraday. Mr Merrick has many interests. But I don't quite see . . . '

'I'm coming to it,' I said. 'He's endowed a museum, I understand.'

'Among other things,' the girl said.

'I'm sure,' I told her.

I stared out to where the blinding white icing-sugar of Merrick's mansion rose from the green wilderness of the park, choosing my words with care. The bulk of the Smith-Wesson made a reassuring pressure against my chest muscles. Henderson had the five slugs from the chambers, it was true. But I still had the spare clip at the bottom of the holster. It always pays to have a second line of defence in my business.

The girl's tones were icy now, as she leaned across the table toward me. I remembered what Henderson had said about her and the estate employees. There was a flush on her cheeks and her breasts rose and fell rapidly beneath the blue silk shirt.

'I don't see where this is getting us, Mr Faraday. What is the point of it all?'

'There is a point, Miss Fallowfield,' I said. 'But I really need to speak to Mr Merrick himself.'

The girl shrugged angrily.

'That's why I'm here, Mr Faraday. To see whether you have a valid reason for seeing Mr Merrick. He rarely gives interviews. You're rather privileged, really. And you're abusing that privilege at the moment.'

Her ritzy manner had me riled up. I looked at my watch in turn.

'We still have forty-five minutes, Miss Fallowfield. Plenty of time for a round table discussion between the three of us.'

A look of intense annoyance passed across the girl's face.

'About what, Mr Faraday?'

'I'm trying to put it as delicately as I can,' I said. 'There doesn't seem to be any means of getting at it without being offensive.'

Susan Fallowfield smiled a tight smile.

'You could try, Mr Faraday.'

I nodded.

'All right. I'm talking about mountain eagles which were shot on this estate. Rare birds which are protected by the government.'

An amazing change had come across the girl's face now. Surprise, shock, suspicion and then rage passed across it in quick succession.

The colour fled from her cheeks, leaving them chalky white. She fought for breath for a few moments. There was fear on her face now as she stared at me. Then she licked her lips and tried to frame her trembling lips to form the sentence.

'I'm afraid I don't understand, Mr Faraday.'

I shook my head.

'It won't wash, Miss Fallowfield. I think you can do better than that.'

'Are you suggesting that Mr Merrick would condone such behaviour on his estate?'

'He's not only condoning it, but I have good reason to believe he shot them himself,' I said.

I traded the girl glance for glance and she turned her eyes down to the terrace, idly scuffing a sandalled foot.

'Let's quit horsing around, Miss Fallowfield,' I said. 'We're talking about something entirely different. It doesn't matter to me what Mr Merrick does up here in private . . . '

The girl had got hold of herself. She burst into my dialogue impetuously.

'You forget yourself, Mr Faraday . . . Mr Merrick's a big man. He can have you thrown out of here. He can do all sorts of things . . . '

'I'm sure he can,' I said mildly. 'But I'm equally sure he would be far too sensible for that. You see I have a client. And I keep records . . . '

The girl half got up from her chair, then thought better of it. I'd got her badly rattled.

'I really don't know what you're talking about, Mr Faraday, or why you're here.'

'Don't you, Miss Fallowfield?' I said.

She lowered her eyes to the ground again.

'Just who is your client, Mr Faraday?'

'That's a professional secret,' I told her.

She bit her lower lip and kept her eyes on the ground.

'And you really expect me to disturb Mr Merrick at an important conference with some wild story about him illegally shooting some protected birds?'

I grinned.

'Hardly. But we both know we're talking about entirely different things. What did you think I was going to do? Denounce him to the S.P.C.A. and have him fined five hundred dollars?'

The Fallowfield number smiled faintly like I'd made a big joke.

'That was rather foolish of me,' she admitted. 'You're a curious man, Mr Faraday. Coming up here alone like this, on to a heavily guarded estate.'

I gave her another long look.

'Are you implying that I'm in some danger here?' I said.

She looked at me, her eyes wide. It was well done but it didn't fool me.

'Good heavens, no, Mr Faraday. Whatever gave you that idea?'

'I'd still like to see Mr Merrick,' I said.

'You're the one who's making a big mystery out of all this.'

The girl bit her lip again.

'I don't know whether he can see you this afternoon.'

'Then he is home?' I said. 'I thought maybe that was his Rolls taking off earlier this afternoon.'

The girl shook her head, her eyes far away.

'Of course he's here, Mr Faraday. Why wouldn't he be? That was probably Mr Dancey, his accountant.'

I raised my eyebrows.

'Nice work if you can get it,' I said.

The girl lifted her eyes again, her attitude more normal. Some of the colour was coming back to her cheeks.

'You won't say who your client is but you accuse Mr Merrick of shooting some legally protected game birds, is that it? What would you have to discuss?'

I lit a cigarette.

'I thought we'd gone over all that,' I said. 'And I figured you for a sensible woman. I want to talk to him. If you mention the game birds he'll know why I want to see him.'

The girl got up and stood frowning down at me. I reached for my pack of cigarettes, lit one and offered them to her. She shook her head.

'I don't think Mr Merrick would have anything to say to you. Good afternoon.'

I shook my head.

'It won't do, Miss Fallowfield. I think Mr Merrick must have a talk with me. If he knows what's good for him.'

She stiffened as though she would have liked to have struck me. I braced myself but the slap never came. She seemed to remember where she was then.

'Are you threatening Mr Merrick. What is this, some sort of blackmail?'

I grinned.

'I thought Mr Merrick was an upright man. What would I have to blackmail him over?'

The Fallowfield number realised her error. She tried to gloss things over. She smiled a stiff smile, like it was painted there and would crack and fall to the ground at any moment.

'You really are the most extraordinary

man, Mr Faraday.'

'You already said that,' I reminded her.

She reached out her hand toward me.

'I think I will have that cigarette now.'

She took it from the pack and I lit it for her. Despite her outward calm her fingers were trembling slightly. I'd struck gold but I didn't quite know how to press home my advantage. She sat down in her chair again, with an easy, elegant movement.

'You must forgive me, Mr Faraday. I'm on edge today. It's not easy being private secretary to a millionaire. Particularly a person like Mr Merrick.'

'Difficult is he?' I said.

The girl nodded.

'You have no idea. The more money and responsibilities people have the more reserved and secretive they become.'

'So I've heard,' I said. 'The Howard Hughes syndrome.'

The girl nodded solemnly, exhaling smoke in a blue cloud which hung around our heads before dispersing in the light breeze.

'So what do you want me to tell Mr

Merrick that would dispose him to talk to you, Mr Faraday?'

'Just two things,' I said. 'Jewellery and money.'

The girl got up like I'd kicked her. She looked physically sick and for a moment I thought she really was going to lay one on me. I looked deep into her eyes and I knew a good deal more about her. I'd won the kewpie-doll all right. I didn't know what the hell the score was but there was something bad in back of it. And Susan Fallowfield was in it right up to her sweet eyeballs.

She had control of herself now.

'Very well, Mr Faraday,' she said at last. 'You've made your point. I think Mr Merrick will see you.'

'You bet he will,' I said.

The girl turned on her heel and started walking down the terrace, leaving a thin swathe of blue smoke in the air behind her.

'Why don't you phone him?' I said. 'It will save you a walk.'

The girl turned then, in a fury of rage. Her shoulders were shaking and her voice was choked.

'I am in charge here, Mr Faraday. What I say goes. And I prefer to speak to Mr Merrick in private about this preposterous story of yours.'

'I'll bet,' I said.

The girl disappeared from the terrace so fast that I hardly saw her go. I sat down again and went on smoking. After a minute or so I strolled over to the edge of the terrace. The girl's figure was a minute speck among the grazing deer. She was running as hard as she could go and already she was up near where the big ornamental staircases bisected the mound leading to the terraces of Merrick's mansion.

I watched until she was out of sight. The birdsong went on and the wind was pleasant and cool after the heat of L.A. The cogs of my mind were working now. I didn't know what I'd stumbled into and I'd have to choose my words with care when Merrick arrived. I didn't think I was in any danger up here but it could be a tricky situation. I'd had to go at things with a sledge-hammer. Trouble was I didn't know what I'd cracked open. Or what unpleasant things would come crawling out from inside.

I went round the guest house, trying all the doors. They were locked and I was certain there was no-one inside. When I was sure I was quite alone I broke out the spare clip from my holster and re-loaded the Smith-Wesson. I went back to the front of the terrace and looked down into the valley.

I grinned. The girl had been gone exactly twelve minutes. Already she was halfway back across the park accompanied by a tall man in a grey light-weight suit. He was half-running too.

13

Merrick bounded lightly up the steps, outwardly calm, but with an air of suppressed anger about him. The girl followed at a more leisurely pace. Merrick shook hands with me perfunctorily and gave me a strained smile.

'This is an odd business, Mr Faraday.'

I nodded.

'You can say that again, Mr Merrick. Sorry to drag you out of your conference like that.'

Merrick looked at me with narrowed eyes, the sun strong on his tanned face. He led the way back to the table the girl had just vacated. He sat down in the chair I'd occupied just as Susan Fallowfield got up to the terrace. She looked bushed. She was as frightened as hell over something and she'd obviously run hard both ways.

I wondered why they hadn't simply used one of the electric buggies or even an automobile but maybe there was some special reason I didn't know about. Merrick waited until the girl had joined us. Then I sat down opposite him at his invitation.

'Miss Fallowfield tells me you're a private detective, Mr Faraday.'

'That's right,' I said.

'I know she's already seen it but I'd like to have a glance at your identification too.'

'By all means,' I said.

I passed the photostat over to him and he studied it in silence while the girl looked uncertainly from me to Merrick and then back to me again.

'This is a rare privilege, Mr Merrick,' I said. 'I'm honoured.'

He gave a thin smile, his face still turned down to my licence details.

'Let's hope you think so by the time this interview's over, Mr Faraday.'

I let that one ride and waited until he'd pushed the document in its plastic folder over to me again. Merrick was a man of about forty-three, with a strong, sun-burned face. He had black, patent-leather hair in which not a trace of grey was showing. His chin was strong, his teeth well-capped and his icy grey eyes were hidden under drooping eyelids which had almost feminine lashes. He had a thick black mustache under his bony nose which gave him a faintly military aspect.

In fact, he looked more like one of Napoleon's cavalry commanders than a modern tycoon and the well-cut grey check suit sat somewhat incongruously upon him as though he'd been born out of his time. Now he folded his strong hands with their well-manicured nails on the table in front of him and studied them frowningly like they were his most important consideration at the moment.

'I think you'd better tell your story again, Mr Faraday,' he said. 'Slowly and clearly with as much detail as possible. From what Susan here tells me, it's fantastic.'

I shrugged.

'It's fantastic, all right. And the implications are fantastic too.'

'I'm not sure I quite understand you, Mr Faraday,' Merrick said blandly.

I gave him one of my best smiles.

'I'm sure you do, Mr Merrick,' I said.

I was beginning to have a screwy feeling about Merrick; the more I thought about the set-up the more unlikely I felt it to be. I leaned forward across the table to him.

'Before we go into all this, there's one thing been puzzling me.'

'Oh, what's that?'

'I understand you're normally almost completely inaccessible to outsiders,' I said. 'Yet as soon as I mentioned these protected birds and the jewellery to Miss Fallowfield here, it brings you on the run.'

There was a sudden sultry atmosphere on the terrace and Merrick looked at me gloweringly; one hard fist on the table in front of him was slowly clenching and unclenching. The girl was staring at him almost imploringly and a glance it was impossible for me to read passed between them. The big man was holding his anger in with difficulty but, perhaps alerted by the look in the secretary's eyes, he turned to me with a shrug.

'Hardly at the run, Mr Faraday. But when it's a matter that concerns my staff or myself and any possible illegality I'm naturally concerned.'

I'd struck him on the raw there. I shook my head.

'I didn't mention anything about illegality, Mr Merrick. And it doesn't concern your staff. It concerns you.'

The big man's fist suddenly clenched again on the table-top.

'You'll have to make yourself more plain, Mr Faraday.'

'I aim to,' I said. 'My problem is to make my position clear without being offensive.'

Before Merrick could reply the girl made a nervous movement of her shoulders. Her voice snapped like a whiplash.

'You needn't concern yourself about that, Mr Faraday. You've already been extremely offensive.'

I held her eyes with my own.

'If I have I'm sorry, Miss Fallowfield. That was hardly my intention. It's my job to get at the truth. And in view of the important position Mr Merrick holds in the world, I thought you'd prefer to do it without scandal or publicity. If possible, that is.'

There was another heavy silence and Merrick's mouth opened once or twice like he was gasping for air.

'You're certainly right there, Mr Faraday,' he said with a nervous laugh. 'But I still don't know what you're driving at.'

I gave him one of my best smiles.

'Only about a hundred and fifty thousand bucks' worth of stolen jewellery,' I said.

*   *   *

I thought Merrick was going to fall apart. The girl's face went chalk-white again. Her glance sought his own but he stared in front of him like he was stunned. He put his big fist in his pocket like he was afraid he might use it on me. His smile was the uneasiest thing I'd seen since J. Carroll Naish and Gene Lockhart were doing it so well in the movies.

'A hundred and fifty thousand dollars?' he repeated mechanically.

'It's a conservative estimate,' I said. 'Maybe more.'

Merrick leaned back in his chair and fixed his eyes somewhere up in the tree-tops. He still couldn't stop the slight trembling of his fingers. I could see them moving beneath the cloth of his jacket pocket.

'This all sounds preposterous,' he said. 'And what it's got to do with me I don't know.'

I shrugged.

'If the stuff's not yours there's an end of it,' I said.

I made as though to get up from the table. He came out of his chair like lightning. He put his big hand very gently on my shoulder. I could feel the trembling of the fingers all right now.

'Please don't let's be hasty, Mr Faraday. Let's talk some more.'

I grinned.

'That's better. I thought you might be interested when I mentioned money.'

Merrick shook his head angrily and sank back into the chair. The girl sat staring in front of her stonily, like she was keeping a tight rein on her feelings.

'You're becoming offensive again, Mr Faraday.'

'That's part of my business too,' I said.

'You're not making sense, Faraday,' he said.

'I think I am,' I said. 'Miss Fallowfield knows something about this stuff. And so do you. I'd like to hear your side of the story before I bring in the official police.'

There was another thunderous pause. Though the sky was still blue it seemed like everything had grown dark up on the terrace. Even the white icing of the distant house looked tarnished.

'Now why would you want to do that, Mr Faraday?' said Merrick softly.

I admired his self-control at that moment. He was handling himself pretty well now.

'If the stuff is stolen . . . ' I said.

He interrupted angrily.

'We don't know that.'

I looked at him through half-narrowed eyelids.

'So you do know something about it.'

He made a convulsive movement with

his arms and shoulders like a puppet who'd suddenly broken a vital part of its machinery.

'It is possible, Mr Faraday. The jewellery may belong to me or Miss Fallowfield here.'

I looked at her steadily.

'Rather an expensive item for a secretary, isn't it?' I said. 'Now, if you'd said your wife or the wife of a business colleague . . .'

Merrick seemed to crumple at the table. He realised his mistake. He bit his lower lip nervously and took his fist out of his jacket pocket again.

'Where is all this leading?' he said.

'You're repeating yourself,' I told him. 'You haven't asked me yet where this jewellery came from or how it got into my hands.'

Merrick's eyes were little pin-points now.

'So you have the stuff, Mr Faraday.'

He saw his mistake too late, swallowed desperately. He cut a pretty poor figure as a millionaire tycoon.

'I mean, Miss Fallowfield has told me

173

all the circumstances as related by you.'

'It won't do, Mr Merrick,' I said. 'You asked me to get to the point just now. The point is you already know all the circumstances surrounding this stuff.'

Merrick's eyes looked trapped and baffled. He stared imploringly at the girl. She stirred herself like she was coming out of a deep sleep.

'It won't hurt you to tell the story again, Mr Faraday.'

'All right,' I said. 'But we're wasting time. Two rare mountain eagles shot on this estate were sent to Vansittart's in L.A. to be treated and mounted up as sporting trophies. They were both protected birds and had been shot illegally. We'll let that pass. But inside the crop of one of them was a diamond necklace and matching earrings. My secretary, who knows something about such things, values them conservatively at around 150,000 dollars. In my book they're stolen property, though I can't prove that.'

Merrick made like he was going to interrupt but I went on as though he wasn't there.

'Before I could get to Vansittart to ask for an explanation someone murdered him. That points at the provenance of the jewellery, wouldn't you have said?'

Merrick blew in his cheeks once or twice.

'This is an appalling story,' he said inanely.

'Isn't it?' I said. 'Not only appalling but inept. The thing has all the hall-marks of amateurs at work. You see, the people who put that stolen stuff in the bird's crop either didn't realise at all or didn't realise in time that he was farming the work out. It could have gone to half a dozen or so specialist firms in this part of California. But the thief or the murderer doesn't know the address.'

'How do you know that?' Susan Fallowfield said sharply.

'Because he broke into Vansittart's office. He escaped without being able to get into the locked file-cabinets that would have given him the information.'

'This is a preposterous story, Mr Faraday,' Merrick said irritably.

'How do you know all this?'

'Because I was there,' I said. 'I got dropped with a karate chop.'

I smiled encouragingly at the girl.

'That's why I carry a gun now.'

I stared thoughtfully at the slightly crumpled figure of the millionaire.

'I figured you might be able to help me. That jewellery does belong to you? Or someone on this estate, doesn't it?'

There was another awkward silence. Merrick looked down in the general direction of his toe-caps. The girl was willing him to say something but he wasn't giving her much help.

'It could be, Mr Faraday,' the Fallowfield number said in a strangled gasp. 'But we'd have to see the stuff.'

'Sure,' I said. 'It's safe in a bank vault for the time being. No doubt we can arrange something.'

I got up. Merrick suddenly flushed and started doing things with his hands and legs. He seemed more like a totally disorganised puppet than ever.

'You mean you want us to come into L.A. and identify it?'

'That's about it,' I said. 'We may have

to get the police in but I'm sure that won't trouble you.'

Merrick clenched his big right fist and put it down carefully on the table top like he was frightened it might get away from him.

'We'll think about it, Mr Faraday.'

'You do that. In the meantime I have a good many things to take care of.'

I gave them a pleasant smile and left them. They sat on at the table in silence. I got over to the phone and called the gate, told Henderson I was ready to go back. When I went down the steps the couple were still sitting under the umbrella like they were figures in the Movieland Wax Museum.

Ten minutes later I was gliding back with the blond character toward the main gate of El Capitan.

14

The blond man said nothing on the way down. His manner seemed to have subtly changed since the outward journey. I wondered if Merrick had phoned fresh orders to the gate. He had had plenty of time because I'd left the terrace straight away. I didn't think anything would happen up here this afternoon but it was as well to be careful. At least I had the Smith-Wesson loaded and ready in case anything broke.

But Henderson didn't make any overt moves; he hadn't even got the shotgun in the sling arrangement on the side of the electric buggy. So I admired the sunshine and the beauties of the estate all the way back while keeping my eyes peeled. The sun shone blandly and nothing happened at all until we whined at last on to the white stone embankment that gave on to the metal bridge.

Henderson switched off and looked at

me. A little bead of perspiration trickled down his hard, sunburnt face.

'Been nice to know you, Mr Faraday,' he said solemnly.

'Likewise,' I said.

He gave me a hard hand to shake. I glanced over at the lodge but it was shuttered and blank-looking against the heat. I walked on toward the bridge. It was winched out all the way to the opposite bank and the sun shone blindingly off the windshield of the Buick on the far side. My footsteps echoed hollow and metallic over the steel plates as I went out toward the middle span, little crawling sensations in the small of my back. When I got to the centre I looked around.

Henderson was standing, a lean, dangerous figure, staring toward me, his shadow stencilled long and black on the dusty ground.

'Drive carefully, Mr Faraday,' he called.

'Sure,' I said. 'I'm always careful in my business.'

He hadn't offered me my five slugs from the Smith-Wesson back so I was on my guard. I walked off the bridge and on to the stone jetty and over toward the Buick without anything happening. I could see another small TV camera atop a post near the edge of the canal had started its silent circling.

I really wanted some time to start digesting what I'd learned this afternoon but this was no place for it. Not that I'd learned a lot but there were many things which didn't fit about the set-up out here. I wound down the windows of the Buick, recoiling from the rush of superheated air and the stink of octane in the baking heat. I waited a couple of minutes to let the breeze penetrate the interior.

I glanced over the canal. The bridge was already rumbling back into the middle island again. Henderson was still standing there, a black, silent monolith as he looked at me through the shimmering waves of heat. The water was like a mirror of molten metal. I didn't hang around any longer but slid behind the wheel, wincing as the heated upholstery seared through my thin shirt. I started the motor and drove slowly round the perimeter of the canal, keeping a sharp eye on the scenery.

Nothing moved in all the wide world except a flight of birds which showed as smudges on the horizon. The TV camera kept circling on its post and I had to resist an impulse to ram the Buick's bonnet at it. Then I gunned on out, back down the way I'd come, the trees again marching at the sides of the private drive, giving welcome shade. My face was a mask of black and white stripes when I looked in the rear mirror.

There was nothing behind me but the faint stirrings of dust from the tyres and now and again the solitary flight of a bird, disturbed from its perch among the bushes. I was back at the big concourse now, the Buick purring along nicely. I still couldn't see any cause for concern but I earned my living and kept on living by being suspicious and I was convinced Merrick and the girl wouldn't leave the matter here. I'd caught them out in something phoney and they'd have to react.

That's what I'd depended on by going out there in the first place. Vansittart's records and Cramp's own conversation were proof that the eagles had originated from Merrick. It was certainly weird though. If the material was stolen — and why should it be hidden like that if it hadn't been — why would Merrick, a millionaire a dozen times over, act so suspiciously this afternoon? It would be crazy to suspect him of stealing it from his own estate; much less that he would be involved in the theft of the stuff from someone else.

The more I knocked it around in my mind the more screwy it seemed. I'd expected Merrick to blow his top and start investigations among his servants and staff. Instead, he'd acted as though he were under suspicion himself. Apart from stalling me off and isolating me from the mansion by meeting me out at the guest-house.

I lit a cigarette and smoked as I drove, the cogs of my mind revolving uselessly; that was where I missed Stella's astringent presence. She would have got to the heart of the matter more quickly and asked more pertinent questions than I was coming up with now. Maybe my brain was getting soggy with the heat this afternoon.

The sun was a little lower but it had lost little of its heat though the breeze was welcome up here. I was in the avenue of poplars and crossed the concourse, the undergrowth hemming in the Buick as I bumped down the narrow lane that led to the estate entrance. The sun was almost dead ahead and becoming a little troublesome, so I lowered the sun visor and concentrated on the steering.

There was nothing and no-one around but I kept my eyes glued to the rear mirror all the way down. Nobody showed and I got up to the triangular strip of tarmac and the thick vegetation which hid the entrance to the main road. I wondered exactly what I'd achieved by going out to El Capitan. Apart from tipping my hand, I mean. But it was difficult to see what else I could have done. I had no more leads and my only approach was to the estate direct.

I had been lucky to see Merrick but now the ball was in his court. I was bait to a certain extent. If the jewellery belonged to him and he wanted it back he would have to approach me. That left the matter of Vansittart's murder. Plus a thousand other questions. I was edging out on to the main road now. I waited, thoughts knocking themselves around endlessly in my mind like free-wheeling billiard balls.

I hung on to let a couple of big fruit-trucks bore on past and then gunned out on to the mountain road, falling in behind and going at a steady pace while I worried at the problems. The sun made striped patterns on the road; the breeze came in cool and comfortable through the windows; the sky had the faintest reddish tinge now as it got on toward later afternoon; and the tyres sang loud and sweetly on the tarmac.

You're getting poetic again, Mike, I told myself. I kept my eyes fixed on the mirror through instinct. I couldn't see anything out of the ordinary. There was a school bus lumbering along now, several hundred yards in rear, and a white sport job in the act of overtaking. It made a harsh, snarling noise in the comparative peace of the afternoon, leaving me standing. The driver must have been all of seventy-five and no doubt thought himself a hell of a fellow.

The tyres screamed as he went into a speed-wobble on the hairpins up ahead and I saw his brake-lights suddenly go on as he closed on one of the fruit-trucks far too quickly. I grinned to myself in the mirror, keeping a wary eye on the three hundred feet drop on my right-hand, separated only by a flimsy-looking white-painted guard rail. The old fool with the over-powered job had got control of his lethal machine by now. I was still watching him when it happened.

An innocent-looking beige coloured saloon had quietly edged up behind and now the driver pulled over and smashed into my rear bumper. The tyres screamed, the steering locked and then I was going toward the guard-rail, eternity just beyond the cliff-edge.

★ ★ ★

Sweat ran into my eyes and blinded me as I wrestled the wheel, the smell of burning rubber filling the Buick's interior as I tentatively gave a touch of brake. The automobile wavered sickeningly, but I had the nose round and corrected the drift, blue smoke from the tyres acrid in my nostrils. For one heart-stopping second the Buick's bodywork touched the guard-rail and than I had bounced back on to the road.

I had my toe down and rocketed on down the bluff, deep anger overlaying the sour taste of fear in my throat. I was angry with myself for being caught offguard like an amateur and angry with the men behind who had so easily almost forced me off the road. The wheelman of the beige saloon had flicked back into the centre of the road with a beautifully controlled movement that denoted the pro.

The saloon kept station about thirty feet in rear, ready for my next move; there was a stream of traffic coming the other way now. Not only did the two men in the beige job not wish to draw attention to themselves but their own manoeuvres were a good deal more dangerous with oncoming traffic. I quickly took out the Smith-Wesson with my disengaged hand, threw off the safety and laid it down on the passenger seat within easy reach.

Perspiration was running down my shirt collar. It had been a near thing. As near as I was likely to get this side the grave. I grinned crookedly, my eyes searching the rear mirror. The sun was clear on the interior of the beige saloon now. The wheelman was a lean, ascetic-looking man with horn-rimmed spectacles. He looked like Arthur Miller on his day off. The man in the passenger seat, nearest me, wore an impeccably tailored white raincoat, despite the heat. He had silver hair and an implacable look about the mouth. If I knew my pros they'd be out of town people hired to do a job and then be flown out again.

The job in this case being to hit me. It was obvious that the man in the passenger seat was the shooter. If the wheelman didn't get me by staging a fake accident, then he'd probably have a shotgun ready to use at the appropriate moment. It would be easy enough up here in the hills where there were plenty of dangerous hairpins and the traffic was normally sparse.

The thought of who might have fingered me flickered momentarily across my mind. This was no time for it though. I'd get to it later. I had only one trump card. The Smith-Wesson. Henderson, the man at Merrick's gateway, knew I'd unloaded it. And he had the shells. He didn't know about the spare clip. I had no doubt that someone at Merrick's estate had put a contract on me. Not me specifically, of course, They couldn't have foreseen my trip up there.

But pros had been at the estate, on tap, and as soon as I'd showed my name had been inked on the contract. The Buick jinked as I hit a rough patch of tarmac and the front wheels wobbled in the direction of the guard-rail again. The beige saloon wasn't doing anything for the moment. The wheelman was biding his time. It was a long way back in to town and there were plenty of ravines where another attempt might be staged.

I got the handkerchief from my pocket and mopped my face. Then I leaned over and wound down my driving window all the way. If I had to shoot there was no sense drilling my own glass. And it might have fatal consequences if I couldn't see properly when the time came. Dust swirled in but the rush of cool air had steadied me and my nerves were back to normal now.

We were going uphill again and I put my foot down on the accelerator, slightly drawing ahead. I knew there was another series of corkscrews the far side of the hill and I wanted to plan out something. If there had been a layby or a roadside café this side, maybe I could have pulled in and made a fight of it. But there was nothing but sheer drops into gorges for miles. These characters had made sure of that. They'd chosen the terrain beautifully and I had no choice but to fight it out.

I was going to try strategy. I'd only use the Smith-Wesson in the last resort. It was a powerful trump card and if they thought I was unarmed they might be tempted to draw alongside to make sure of their target. In which case I'd be well-placed. But it would be a war of nerves and mine were wearing a little thin already.

The beige saloon was drawing up now. The Buick was no match for it. There was obviously a souped-up engine from a more powerful automobile under that innocuous-looking bonnet. I studied the driver in the rear mirror. His face was set like rock. I shifted to his companion. The man with silver hair was rummaging down somewhere below the edge of the window. He was obviously fitting his kit together.

A specially modified shotgun with a demountable stock; extremely useful in a getaway when the two halves can be hung from the belt and worn under a raincoat while the law is looking for a man carrying a heavy piece. The shotgun is the method favoured by professional hitmen. It has a wide spread at close range and is guaranteed to take its target out. That's the theory at any rate. And nine times out of ten it's true.

I looked at the wheelman again and then shifted back to the man in the passenger seat. He was well over sixty, I should have said; a veteran pro whose steady nerve had maybe taken him through a couple of hundred killings in a long career. How did I know all this? I knew all right. The ramming of my fender was a scientifically calculated opening shot that would have taken most drivers out.

That it hadn't taken me was no thanks to my intuition or driving skill. It was the sheerest good fortune. But I was on guard now and I didn't aim to be at a disadvantage again. I was in the middle of my lane, keeping the rails and the cliff-edge well away. He'd have to hit me broadside this time to force me off and I would have a chance to use the Smith-Wesson if he did.

It had rolled to one side of the passenger seat and I reached out with my right hand to pull it back. I took my eyes off the mirror to do that and as I did so I heard the snarl of the motor of the souped-up job behind. The man who was making that move had incredible eyes that could see a fly's antennae at fifty paces. I was exaggerating, of course. But it was that sort of vision.

I know he was wearing glasses but I guessed they were probably for disguise. The people who carried out these jobs often used distinctive types of spectacles, often with plain glass in the lenses. Most wheelmen certainly don't rise in their profession from the ranks of people with weak eyes. And they are professionals in a demanding profession. I knew that because I'd been on the receiving end more than once.

I was already steering farther over and had my toe down on the accelerator but the Buick was no match for the beige saloon. I saw its bonnet looming in the mirror. But I hadn't done so badly because the blow on the fender was a glancing one and it merely sent me forward. There was nothing else on the highway for the moment so it was open house. I was getting angrier now so I turned my wheel sharply to the left, steering into the path of the saloon which was just dropping back.

It was pretty suicidal but it was an intemperate reaction and I relied on the expertise of the wheelman to take us both out of a wipeout situation. I heard the tyres screaming at the road and saw the saloon jinking crazily in the mirror. I showed my teeth at its reflection as it did three incredible curves in the centre lane of the highway. I heard a horn blare then and saw a big refrigerator truck coming the opposite way.

The man driving the big saloon was under control and he went back into the nearside lane like he was radio-controlled. The expression on his face hadn't changed. There was nothing personal in all this. It was just a job to him. It was probably getting boring because the quarry wouldn't co-operate. I guessed the hitman would be brought in pretty soon.

We couldn't keep this up and he'd be running out of ravine in another ten minutes. My face was streaked with perspiration and the dust drifting in the window was choking me. I saw a big layby coming up on the opposite side of the road. It had a fruit-stand and a couple of ice-cream concessions and there were a lot of children and elderly tourists standing around.

I had been debating whether to pull over to the offside if I could find a gap but decided against it now. I didn't mind risking my own life but it was unfair to involve children and geriatrics. Those I missed on my way down the layby were bound to be struck by the man driving the saloon. I saw he had weighed it up himself because the snout of his vehicle was coming up incredibly fast. He kept about two feet behind me until it was too late for me to pull over.

The white-haired man straightened up now. I could see the glint of something metallic just showing over the lower edge of the window. He obviously couldn't shoot through the door-panel so I'd get plenty of warning when he intended to make his play. I figured he would have to come alongside to take me out. That would be the moment to make my move.

I reached for the Smith-Wesson and put it in my lap. When the moment came

I'd use my right and steer with my left. I would have to sight over my left wrist through the open window, which was a little restrictive. But I figured at the range we'd be operating and by pumping the whole set of shells I'd be able to manage something spectacular.

If he kept behind and went for my tyres that would be a wholly different ball-game altogether. I kept my eyes on the mirror. He'd dropped back fifteen or twenty feet and was keeping out in the offside lane. We were on another series of ess-bends now and the view here was even more spectacular. It had to be now because we were coming to a cutting and there would be nothing but a rock wall at my right hand soon which would be useless for their purposes.

I figured they would still go for the accident if they could manage it. White-hair was just getting ready like all first-rate professionals. He would leave the decision to the wheelman. If he failed then white-hair would take over and the driver would work on instructions from him. There was a correct protocol in such matters.

The last of the opposing traffic drifted away in a tangled skein in my mirror. There was nothing else on the road behind us except a big blue car towing a caravan which was a long way back. It disappeared and a few seconds later I heard the howling snarl of the souped-up motor. The beige saloon was pulling out and coming up alongside, the face of the driver solemn and concentrated.

The sunlight glinted on his spectacles and on the barrels of the shotgun white-hair was poking through the passenger window. I accelerated up and then braked slightly. It was a risky business but they overshot and I could see the white-haired man say something through set teeth at the driver. I accelerated again while the beige saloon was braking and pulled up slightly in rear while the hitman was still thinking about his priorities.

The barrel was facing forward and he couldn't bring it to bear. I raised the Smith-Wesson and got off two quick shots. The windscreen of the saloon starred and I saw the wheelman slump, blood spattering the car interior. The screen looked like it was raining blackberry juice. The white-haired man leaned over and clawed at the wheel as the saloon started to do crazy things.

I was braking again now and got off two more shots; one must have found a tyre because the big car slewed at an insane angle, smoke coming from the bonnet. Whitehair had turned now. He got off one shot which tore a big hole in the tarmac in front of the Buick. I got down behind the wheel and braked harder, the white railing coming up dangerously close.

The saloon was in front of me, in my own lane now, going like mad. It tore away a whole section of the white railing and soared twenty feet out into the valley below. Whitehair got off a last shot while he was still in the air. It probably reached Santa Monica because it came nowhere near me.

I'd stopped now and watched in disbelief. The saloon kept on going for a long time. Then it disappeared in a belt of dark pines. The explosion came up curiously muffled. Then there were great tongues of crimson flame and a pall of black smoke that made a mushroom-shaped cloud over the tree tops. I got out the Buick and leaned against the rail and gulped in air. I found I was trembling. I saw a fruit-truck had stopped on the opposite shoulder. The driver, a big red-faced man with ginger hair and dressed in green coveralls came pounding over. His eyes glazed as he stared down into the valley.

'Jesus Christ,' he said softly.

He turned back to me, his eyes not seeing me.

'I saw the whole thing. What the hell were they trying to do?'

'I think they were on their way to a cremation,' I said.

15

'You gave them a rough ride, Mike,' Stella said.

I blew out a column of fragrant blue smoke and frowned at the cracks in the ceiling.

'They asked for it,' I said.

It was turned six now and I'd just found Stella packing up for the day. She'd gone pale under her tan as I filled her in on the details but her pen went on steadily scratching across the paper as she took notes.

'So where do we go from here?' she said.

I reached out for my coffee cup, watching the reddening sun at the window blinds.

'I threw down a challenge and they picked it up,' I said.

Stella shivered suddenly like she was cold.

'You're staking yourself out,' she said.

'It was all I could do,' I said. 'I decided to level with Merrick and hope that something would break.'

'You think he sent those men to take you out, Mike?'

Stella's eyes were very blue over the rim of her cup.

'It was obvious,' I said. 'I had him bugged all the time I was up there. There's something more behind this than stolen diamonds and illegal eagles.'

Stella made an elegant little snorting noise.

'I should have thought that was obvious. Otherwise, why kill Vansittart? Why try to kill you?'

I shook my head, watching my cigarette smoke rising in slow whorls toward the ceiling.

'I mean more even than that. I didn't have much technical conversation with him but Merrick didn't strike me as the type who would be interested in ornithology anyway.'

Stella caught my eyes with her own, held them.

'Don't you find that significant, Mike?' she said gently.

'It probably is,' I said. 'But I feel too beat-up for the moment to exactly grasp its significance.'

Stella picked up her cup and came over from her desk. She sat down in the client's chair opposite me and swung a long, elegant leg.

'Try this for size, Mike,' she said. 'Supposing Merrick is tied up with the girl. She's his mistress from what you say.'

'That seemed pretty obvious from what the gateman said.'

Stella shrugged.

'Suppose they can't afford to have anyone know about the jewellery.'

'That's equally obvious,' I said.

Stella tossed the gold bell of her hair back from her eyes.

'You miss my point, Mike,' she said drily. 'Supposing the jewellery belonged to Merrick's wife. Supposing he and this Susan Fallowfield had murdered her somewhere up on the estate and were salting all her property away.'

I sat upright in my swivel chair, the cogs of my mind racing.

'It's an interesting theory, honey,' I

said. 'It still doesn't sit right but you've got something.'

Stella looked at me and said nothing.

'In the first place, Merrick isn't married, according to the record. Secondly, he's divorced. Thirdly, why would a millionaire want to steal jewellery he'd probably bought in the first place; could have paid for a hundred times over; and above all, why would he want to smuggle it out of his own estate in the craw of an eagle?'

'Crop, Mike,' Stella said absently.

'It sticks in my craw, anyway,' I said.

She didn't bother to answer that, just went on sitting opposite, puzzling away at whatever strand of thought she'd gotten hold of.

'Even so,' I said. 'There's a lot in what you say. There's something that Merrick and the girl daren't risk the outside world knowing about.'

'Let's get back to the Vansittart kill,' Stella said. 'Why would they want to take him out?'

'Assuming it's Merrick and the girl,' I said. 'Because they wanted the address where the eagle had been sent. Something went wrong. Like I said, they're amateurs.'

Stella sat back, her hands cupped round one tanned knee, her eyes glinting.

'Exactly, Mike. Why would they want to kill you if you were the only person who could lead them to the stolen jewellery?'

I looked at her for a long moment, the cogs of my mind moving into high gear. It had gotten very quiet in the office. I checked my watch. It was almost a quarter of seven now and neons were beginning to prick the dusk outside the window. I shook my head, feeling the weight of the Smith-Wesson in its nylon harness. I still had one slug in the chamber.

'I'd learned too much,' I said. 'I was on to them. But you're wrong about one thing. I wasn't the only person who knew about the stuff. I told them you had put a tentative value on it.'

I got up from the desk and took Stella's hand, pulling her to her feet.

'You'd better go out the back way and don't hang around,' I said. 'Have you got somewhere you can stay tonight without going home?'

Stella put up her hand and patted a hair into place in her immaculate coiffure.

'Have you gone crazy, Mike?'

I shook my head.

'I was never more sane, honey. They'll come for you because they know a girl will be easier to deal with. That's why they didn't care about taking me out. They'll make you get that stuff out the bank vault and after they've got it they'll kill you.'

Stella stared at me in the heavy silence. She had a tight, defiant little smile on her lips.

'But you won't let them, Mike, will you?'

I held her close to me.

'Not in a thousand years,' I said.

* * *

I sat on at the desk, smoking my third cigarette. It was almost eight now. I figured they wouldn't come until after eight. They'd maybe stake Stella's place out first. Then they'd come here. Principally because they wouldn't know anywhere else to go. So I'd left the desk light on to help them.

I'd taken Stella out the back way and made sure there was no-one around. I'd seen her drive off before I'd gone back in again. I was getting hungry now. I hoped they wouldn't be too long because I wanted to eat.

I knew they'd be along. Mainly because even though the two men in the beige saloon couldn't report back to them, Merrick and the girl might assume that the job had been done. They were amateurs, after all. So they wouldn't expect to find me sitting here. They'd maybe think Stella was working late. I had to set the scene before then but I had plenty of time, because I'd either hear the elevator coming up or some sound from the corridor outside my office.

So I sat on, drinking a little of the bourbon from the half-bottle in my desk. I was certain they'd be here. If they'd driven in they'd have seen the hole in the fence and the ambulance men and the police cars. It might be days before anyone could identify the charred remains of white-hair and his companion. So I thought it fairly certain that the people at El Capitan estate would assume that everything had gone according to plan. Whatever that was.

I watched the neons through the window blinds, listening to the heavy thumping of my heart, the muted traffic noises from the street below and feeling the coolness of the night wind on my cheek from the half-open window. I glanced at my watch again and then got up from my desk. I went over to Stella's. She had a couple of files out earlier and I guessed one of them would contain her typed notes of Abel Cramp's little problem.

There were several newspaper cuttings she'd dug up from somewhere and I picked them up idly and glanced through them. I stiffened, the traffic noises blurring away, the taste of the bourbon on my tongue receding. The heading was: Millionaire Recluse Donates Museum to City. There was a picture of Merrick with his third wife. It was a fine, clear picture and I stared at it uncomprehendingly.

I was still standing there staring at the thing when I heard a faint, slurring footfall in the corridor. I got the Smith-Wesson out the holster and transferred it to my right-hand trousers pocket. I left the desk light on and got over to the waiting room door which I'd left ajar. The waiting room was in darkness. I just had time to make it. I got in the deepest shadow in rear of the door when a heavy shadow stencilled itself across the frosted glass.

The door opened quietly and a bulky figure edged itself through. I had my finger on the trigger of the Smith-Wesson. Not that that would have helped because I had the safety on. But it felt a little better after my experiences this afternoon. The man in the white lightweight raincoat and the green pork-pie hat hesitated. He had a back that was as broad as a subway carriage and I didn't aim to tangle with him without the Smith-Wesson.

I could see the details of the character's

clothing and the hat clearly enough by the light coming in from the corridor through the frosted glass of the door but the face was in deep shadow. Green-hat moved very quietly over toward the doorway and peeked through. He stood there for a few seconds as though his eyes were adjusting to the lowered intensity of the lighting.

I crossed the intervening space between us as quietly as I could. I had the Smith-Wesson out now, the safety off. I held the piece up ready. The man in the white raincoat opened the door slowly and stepped through into my office. I was getting tired of the drama.

'Looking for someone?' I said.

The character must have had strong nerves because he didn't move though my question must have been a shock. But there was the slightest hunching of the shoulders. The figure didn't turn around but merely said quietly:

'Ah, Mr Faraday. Just the man I was looking for.'

It was my turn to be surprised. I lowered the gun slowly as the figure turned round, taking off the hat. I took in the grim face and the shock of grey hair.

'I took the liberty of coming up when I saw your light burning.'

I didn't recognise her at first, then my brain was working properly again.

'Miss Parker, isn't it? From Vansit-tart's?'

'That's it, Mr Faraday. I want to see you about something important.'

'Come on in. You must forgive the gun but I've had a trying day.'

The massive woman preceded me into the office and sank into the client's chair at my invitation. I went around the desk and put the Smith-Wesson back in my holster. I looked at the Parker woman carefully. Her face looked worn and worried beneath the dim light of the desk lamp.

'Would you like a drink?' I said. 'I was just having one myself. Afraid it's only bourbon.'

'Bourbon will be fine, Mr Faraday.'

I went over to the water-cooler and got two paper cups. I filled them half and half whisky and water and carried them back. The Parker woman picked up hers and took a deep gulp. I went to sit down again and studied her face.

'I needed that, Mr Faraday. It's been quite a time at Vansittart's too, I can tell you. The tragedy of Giles' murder and then this break-in. The place has been swarming with police.'

'I can imagine,' I said.

I sat back in my chair and swivelled the bourbon around on my tongue.

'Has something else happened? Is that why you're here?'

The Parker woman nodded, taking another gulp at her paper cup.

'Miss King was worried too. That's why I had to come and see you.'

'She's all right?' I said.

The big woman nodded. Her eyes were a curious slatey colour and this, combined with her grim expression and her massive build made her a formidable figure. The chair creaked with her weight as she shifted ponderously into a more comfortable position. Her ashen-grey hair was almost brutally cut back from her face and she looked more like a Joe Stalin poster than ever. What I hadn't realised before was her tremendous physique.

She had hands like ham-bones which hung loosely down from the sleeves of her raincoat and as she stared at me across the desk, the two deep lines that ran each side of her nose and down to the edges of her mouth looked like cracks in the façade that she presented to the world.

Her face was lightly tanned by the sun which gave it an unattractive yellow appearance and there were white patches underneath the cold, slate-grey eyes. She had a big nose and when she opened her greyish lips she revealed nicotine-stained teeth.

She was so unattractive that she almost succeeded in converting it into a virtue. She must have been around fifty-five; at the same time she conveyed the impression that she was a good deal younger and also a good deal older. The youthful side came from the powerful physique; the older side from the grey hair and the lines on her face. I gave up beating my brains out over it. I had other things to think about tonight. The Parker woman stirred in her chair.

'Miss King is fine, Mr Faraday. But something has come up at the office. It's connected with the break-in. I thought you ought to know about it.'

I nodded.

'I'm grateful.'

The Parker woman was rummaging about in her raincoat pocket with her big, clumsy-looking hands. She looked annoyed.

'I've come out without my cigarettes, Mr Faraday. Could you oblige?'

'Sure,' I said.

I got out my pack and leaned across the desk toward her. She got up and bent down, reaching out with her left for the proffered smoke. That was when her right hand, big as a T-bone steak came round in a blurred arc that had all the crushing impact of a sledge-hammer. I went out so quick I wasn't even aware of it.

16

I tasted blood. There was a singing in my ears and a rocking motion that made me feel worse. I opened my eyes, found I could see after a fashion. My mouth felt like the bottom of a waste bin after Fourth of July celebrations. The singing cleared and I could hear a motor working then. That and the rocking motion led me to the conclusion that I was in an automobile travelling somewhere.

But where? I could focus my eyes a little now. I was lying on the floor of the vehicle because I was getting the drumming of the transmission close to my ears. Dust tickled my nostrils and I could make out some sort of heavily textured carpet a few inches in front of my face.

I closed my eyes again and played possum. The gears were changing and we were jolting uphill. I lifted my head very slightly in the deep shadow beneath the seat. From under my eyelids I could see the accelerator and brake pedals of the vehicle. A huge foot in a woman's mannish brogue was clamped down heavily on the accelerator.

There was no doubt Miss Parker was doing the driving. A number of questions came to mind but I shoved most of them to the back of what was left of my brain. After a preliminary report on my physical condition, the first thing I wanted to know was whether Parker was alone. Not that it would have helped me much. I was all beat up and from what I had seen of her she could have handled one of the Red Army's front-line battalions on her own, let alone me.

So I kept a low profile in both senses of the term and sweated it out, quietly flexing my limbs and finding in a few minutes that I was more or less in one piece. The woman certainly packed a punch though. I guessed then that she was the one who'd chloroformed Karen King and done a karate operation on me at Vansittart's office. I should have got to it sooner but I was acting even dumber than usual on this case.

With the knowledge I now had it became even more obvious that Ma Parker was ninety-nine per cent responsible for the death of Vansittart. He'd had his neck broken by a murderous chop limited usually to karate experts. Parker didn't need to be a karate expert with her build and the ham-bones she used for hands. She could have taken my head off if she'd had a mind to.

I was glad it had been me and not Stella. I guessed now Parker was taking me somewhere to keep me on ice overnight. Then tomorrow I might be persuaded to give up the bank details so that she or the Fallowfield girl could retrieve the jewellery. There was no doubt now that all of the three: Merrick, the girl and the Parker woman were tied up together. But how or why was a different matter. There were a dozen threads I hadn't yet got but the smoke was beginning to clear.

I put my head back on the matting and closed my eyes again. I must have dozed for a few minutes because when I came awake again the note of the motor had changed. We were idling gently along very rough surfaces, still going uphill. I had no way of knowing how long I'd been out but I calculated maybe an hour.

I knew now there was no-one but Parker and me in the car because I hadn't heard the slightest hint of conversation or anything that would indicate the presence of anyone else in the vehicle. The woman had some nerve though. She must have carried me like a sack of potatoes down to the ground floor of my building and out to the car. That took some strength as well as some cool. Because I'm no lightweight.

It also created something like a record in my cases. It was the first time I'd had a female opponent of this weight and class. I hoped I'd survive the next round to be able to enter it in my files. Though I hadn't a hope of going the full contest with her. Even Cumberland style. I smiled faintly, feeling the side of my head was going to fall off. I gave up the humour and concentrated on the serious side of the situation. Which wasn't very difficult.

'You're awake now, eh?'

The Parker number leaned over me like an Amazon woman who was just about to give the coup de grace to a fallen warrior.

'Just about,' I admitted.

My voice came out as a hoarse croak. The Parker woman sniggered.

'You're pretty tough, Mr Faraday,' she said. 'When I hit them they usually stay out four or five hours.'

'When they don't go out altogether,' I said.

She laughed throatily with a sound that was like a cold wind blowing through rusty sheet iron.

'You're good, Mr Faraday. A real pro.'

'So are you,' I said.

I was trying to get up now and she took me by the collar with one of her ham-bone hands and lifted me effortlessly, throwing me into the passenger seat. I almost passed out again but sat there stitching my thoughts together while I fought for breath.

'What happened to Saatchi and Steevens?' she said.

'If you mean the wheelman and the

white-haired shotgun artist, they went over the cliff,' I said.

I was facing toward her now and I opened my eyes again. She was hunched bare-headed over the wheel, concentrating on the steering, her lips a hard, thin line.

'They were good too,' she said. 'That means you must be better.'

She shot me a glance in which respect was mixed with venom.

'Why did you get mixed up with all this, Mr Faraday?'

'It's my job, Miss Parker,' I said.

She screwed up her mouth, turning the car with easy, skilful movements over the pot-holes. There were no lights anywhere so I guessed we were a long way from L.A. I shot a quick glance at my watch. I'd been out just over the hour, like I figured. I have an instinct about such things. Which can be useful. I would need a lot of useful information tonight if I were to come out in one piece. I tried to ignore the little bearded men who were beating a tattoo on my skull with iron slicing bars and concentrated on the

Parker woman's dialogue.

'It's my job to get that jewellery back,' she said.

'What jewellery?' I said.

She laughed the grating laugh again.

'Come on, Mr Faraday. We both know what we're talking about.'

I stared at her unlovely profile. I wondered whether I might chance going out the passenger door. We weren't travelling very fast at the moment. On the other hand it was probably locked and if I couldn't find the catch in the dark I'd be cold in a split-second. Apart from the fact that she'd probably grab me before I'd even halfway made my move. She had fantastic reflexes. I decided to forget it.

'The stuff's in the bank,' I said.

She nodded approvingly.

'We know that too. We're going down to get it first thing in the morning.'

'That's what I figured,' I said.

I slewed a little in my seat and studied her carefully. The pain was receding from my head now but my neck muscles were throbbing nicely.

'You mind if I smoke?'

'Go ahead.'

She chuckled again.

'You needn't bother about looking for the Smith-Wesson. I have it here. It's still got one slug in it.'

'I wouldn't have dreamt of going for it,' I said. 'Do you think I couldn't tell by the weight of the harness that it had gone?'

The Parker woman nodded her head like I'd said something profound.

'I guess you'd have to be pretty dumb, even for a private dick, not to notice.'

I reached in carefully and found my pack. The cigarettes had been squashed flat when I hit the floor of my office but I straightened them out with fingers that were far from steady. Before I could get one to my mouth her massive, spatulate fingers were in front of my nose with the dashboard lighter

'You're a real lady,' I said.

She cleared her throat with a rasping noise, replacing the lighter in the dash fitting.

'You'd be surprised, Mr Faraday. I can be pleasant when I like. Just don't upset me. People always regret it when I turn nasty.'

I feathered out blue smoke and looked at the dark nothingness through the windshield. There was only the rutted, unmade road in the yellow light of the headlamps.

'I can imagine,' I said. 'I'm not too fond of your tantrums myself.'

She smiled reflectively. It didn't do anything for her looks though.

'I had to make sure of you, Mr Faraday. I knew you carry firearms and I couldn't take a chance.'

'How did you get me out?' I said.

The big woman shrugged, her ash-grey hair slightly stirring in the breeze that was coming in through the driving window.

'Carried you. What did you think? No-one's going to notice a guy carrying a drunk home in a city like L.A.'

'You're right,' I said. 'I just thought I'd ask to help the conversation along.'

There was silence for a few moments; I was no longer conscious of the noise of the car-engine and the creaking of the springs. I found myself drifting off again.

This dame sure knew how to hit.

'What about Miss King?' I said. 'She all right?'

The Parker number grunted.

'No reason why she shouldn't be. She knows nothing about all this, if that's what you mean.'

She gave another grunt, of satisfaction this time, and pulled the big car around. She steered it through two pillars made from blocks of natural stone.

'We're here, Mr Faraday. Just behave yourself or I'll have to put you out again.'

* * *

Miss Parker stopped the car in front of a large frame bungalow without lights and killed the motor. The silence crowded in, broken only by the distant sighing of the wind and the croaking of frogs. The big woman switched off the headlamps but kept the sidelights burning. My Smith-Wesson had suddenly appeared in her massive right fist. She motioned me out the car.

I almost fell as I quitted the passenger

seat. I must have been more beat-up than I thought. I ground out my cigarette beneath my heel.

'Where are we, Happy Valley?' I said.

The big woman smiled grimly.

'Somewhere private, Mr Faraday. Where we can hole up nicely until morning.'

'It sounds an alluring prospect,' I said.

She reached in the driver's seat and killed the sidelights.

'No sense in advertising our presence,' she said.

I looked around the wilderness of garden. The place was overgrown and my guess was the house hadn't been used for years. No other lights pricked the darkness so we must be in a secluded spot. Yet it couldn't have been too far from L.A. because it had only taken just over an hour to get out here.

'After you, Mr Faraday,' she said politely.

I went ahead up the bare cement steps which were thickly overgrown with moss and lichen. I had a job to keep my footing and my head had started aching again. I waited while she fumbled with the key in the shabby front door. She kept the Smith-Wesson steady on my gut.

'It only needs one bullet, Mr Faraday,' she said significantly.

'So I've been told,' I said.

I waited while she opened up the door. The hall inside was dark and gloomy, with only faint light coming in from the sky. She closed the door behind us and latched it.

'It's an old property that belonged to my family,' she said.

'You disappoint me,' I said. 'I thought you were doing an article for Good Housekeeping.'

A match flared, giving out a bright yellow light. It made heavy caverns of the Parker woman's eyes.

'Spare me the humour, Mr Faraday,' she said ponderously. 'It won't get you out of this.'

'Maybe not,' I said. 'But it helps to pass the time.'

She didn't answer that, just put the match to the wick of a big oil lamp that was standing on an occasional table in the hall. She trimmed it with a grunt of satisfaction, turning the brass wheel until it was burning brightly. Then she replaced the glass globe. All the time her right hand held the gun steady. The dim yellow light shone on damp, discoloured walls and peeling wallpaper.

'In here, Mr Faraday.'

She opened up a facing door and pushed me through, coming in behind me carrying the lamp. She put it down on a dusty pine mantelpiece and went over to light another one that was standing on a table in the middle of the room. The light made the place seem a little more cheerful but it still wouldn't have made House Beautiful.

I sat down on a sagging divan and stared at the decor.

'I'd like another cigarette,' I said.

She nodded. 'Go ahead.'

She came forward into the centre of the room, a formidable figure, her hambone hands hanging stiffly at her sides. The Smith-Wesson was still dangling from her right so I didn't try anything.

'What happens now?' I said.

'We wait, Mr Faraday.'

'I hope you've got something for us to eat,' I said. 'It's likely to be a long haul until morning.'

She nodded ponderously.

'It's been taken care of.'

Her eyes flickered round the room with satisfaction. She went over to pull the thick, dusty drapes over the two windows. One was in the side wall and the other set, a pair of French doors, gave on to the garden, I figured. Or what was left of it. She came back and stood looking down at me.

'If you want to use the john it's through that door there.'

There was a little glint of malicious humour struggling in back of her eyes.

'It doesn't lead anywhere so don't think you can get out. The window's not only high up but small. Far too small for you to get through.'

She hefted the Smith-Wesson, her voice becoming soft and dreamy. Leastways, as soft and dreamy as a voice like hers could get.

'Apart from that it's got iron bars over it.'

'Thanks for telling me,' I said. 'If I need it during the course of the night I'll put up my hand.'

I got out my sagging pack again and lit up. I put my spent match-stalk back in the box. The Parker woman went to sit in the ruin of an old leather chair. She glanced at a watch as big as a pancake that was strapped to her wrist with what looked like ship's cable. Like everything else about her it was wildly out of scale with normal life.

'It's damp in here, Mr Faraday,' she said. 'Make yourself useful by building a fire. There's wood and paper in the scuttle over yonder.'

'If you think you can trust me,' I said.

She nodded.

'I can trust you.'

I got up and walked rather unsteadily over toward the fireplace. I had to pass her to get there. As I went by her foot came out with astonishing swiftness. I had no time to avoid it. I felt a numbing pain in my ankle. I went down on my face with a crash that shook the building. I felt angry and winded. The Parker woman's tittering seemed to fill the whole of the bungalow.

'That's just so you don't get any ideas, Mr Faraday.'

The muzzle of the Smith-Wesson looked as big as the mouth of an L.A. freeway tunnel.

'I haven't got any ideas, Miss Parker,' I said. 'My brain's too scrambled for that.'

I got up, fighting for breath, dragging myself forward with my hands. I almost passed out again. When my head was clearer I found the old brass scuttle she'd spoken about. I picked up my smouldering cigarette butt and coaxed a piece of paper into flame. I screwed up several newspapers and made a sizeable blaze on the rusty iron firebasket. I fed it chips of dry wood and then put the bigger stuff on top.

In about half an hour I had a respectable log fire going, the flames flickering nicely on the walls and ceiling and competing with the lamplight. It certainly did a lot to get rid of the musty odour. It was around ten o'clock by the time I'd finished and the big woman sat watching me in silence, occasionally taking a drag from a hip-flask in the pocket of her raincoat.

She'd kept it on all the time we were in the house and my Smith-Wesson sat on the brim of her pork-pie hat on a small table at her side, where she could get at it in a hurry. I walked over toward her, keeping well out of range of her feet. I was still limping a little and that seemed to amuse her.

'Why did you kill Vansittart?' I said.

The corners of her mouth turned down and her shoulders hunched. She was a formidable figure sitting there and I stepped back a little.

'That's not one of the things up for discussion, Mr Faraday,' she said.

I grinned.

'Just how do you think you're going to get the stuff tomorrow? Do you expect me to go in the bank and ask for it?'

She nodded slowly.

'That's exactly what we expect, Mr Faraday.'

I shook my head.

'I don't think so.'

The big woman got up. She looked at me seriously.

'I think so, Mr Faraday.'

Something like a tree branch caught me beneath the chin. I cart-wheeled through the air and slammed up against the wall. Before I could move she had me in the gut with her left. My breath whistled out with a noise that even to me sounded shocking. As I sagged she kneed me in the groin. Some woman. I must have passed out again then.

When I came around the fire was burning low and the Parker number was feeding it with logs.

She came over and lifted me with one hand. She threw me effortlessly into the big leather chair. I bounced and her massive right hand pinned me, held me there. She forced the neck of the flask into my mouth. I felt the raw spirit trickle through my teeth. I felt warmed and better then. She grunted and stood back, her head cocked like she was listening for something.

'You're a fool, Mr Faraday. Why don't you take notice of what I tell you?'

'You never tell me the right things,' I said.

She frowned down at me in her best Russian commissar manner.

'Like I said, Mr Faraday, we're going down to the bank tomorrow and you're going to do exactly as you're told.'

'Check,' I said. 'That's what I was going to say earlier but you didn't give me time to get around to it.'

She stood there frowning in the lamplight like she found me hard to make out.

'You're a real pro, Mr Faraday. And you're tough all right. But you're a fool, just the same.'

'Maybe,' I said.

She shook the ashen-grey hair vigorously.

'No maybe about it. We can kill you, sure. But if we don't get what we want from you we merely start on your little blonde secretary. You wouldn't want that, would you?'

I shook my head, tasting blood again.

'I wouldn't want that, Miss Parker,' I said. 'Leave her out of it.'

The big woman cracked her fingers with a noise that sounded like a series of pistol shots in the quiet bungalow.

'So long as you play ball.'

I nodded, half afraid the front of my face would fall off. I could feel blood crusted on the side of my head.

'I'll play ball, Miss Parker.'

'Good.'

We were still like that when there was the noise of a car coming up the road outside and yellow headlamp beams shone flickering through the drapes at the side-windows.

17

The big woman shifted over to the door, her head down, listening intently. The Smith-Wesson was back in her massive fist again.

'Don't move,' she said in her rusty tin voice.

'You must be joking,' I said.

She passed, a dark shadow between the oil lamps, her silhouette monstrous and elongated on the ceiling. I tried to get up, fell back against the leather padding of the chair. I heard the lock on the front door rasp back and the low mumble of voices.

More shadows crawled in the doorway. I fished for another cigarette, put it between my lips. I felt a little better then though the scene had a tendency to recede. Someone was still playing a Bach gavotte on my skull with sledgehammers. The Parker woman didn't know her own strength.

'So we meet again, Mr Faraday,' the girl said.

She came forward into the golden arc of the lamplight and smiled down at me. She wore a white raincoat and looked as innocent and fresh as a day in spring.

'I'll bet you didn't expect that,' I said.

She came over and looked critically at my beat-up face.

'I see you've been getting together with Miss Parker.'

'That's right,' I said. 'I'll bet she's pretty good at lacework and tatting too.'

Susan Fallowfield gave me a bright glance. She seemed a little more sure of herself than when we'd last met. But then she had reason to be. The glowing end of a cigarette materialised from out the shadow behind her. Merrick came over and looked at me blandly. He still wore the grey suit and he carried a big automatic pistol in his fist. He sighed.

'You've given us a lot of trouble, Mr Faraday.'

'I'm real sorry about that,' I said.

I eased myself up in the chair, found the buzzing in my head had stopped.

Merrick bent over and examined the side of my face. He whistled through his teeth.

'You'd better fix that up, Susan,' he told the girl.

He turned to the big woman, who stood sullenly in the middle of the room. The atmosphere had subtly changed now.

'You should learn to take it easy, Ma,' he said gently. 'We want Mr Faraday in good condition for the bank tomorrow.'

The grey-haired woman put the Smith-Wesson casually back into the pocket of her raincoat. She went over to stand looking down into the fire.

'There's no permanent damage,' she said. 'Mr Faraday's a very durable character.'

Merrick grunted. He put his automatic on a table in the centre of the room. He disappeared into the shadow and came back with a blue canvas holdall. He started putting stuff down on the table; a couple of thermos flasks, plastic cups, sandwiches packed in cellophane. The girl had left the room while he was doing that.

Now she came back with a bowl of cold water, some soap and a clean towel she'd found somewhere. She leaned over me and started gently sponging the caked blood away from the side of my head. I must have collected that when I collided with the wall. Or maybe it was when the Parker woman first laid me out in the office. I seemed to have been acting as a punchbag all evening. It might have been weeks since she'd come to my office though it couldn't have been more than four or five hours in reality. The girl winced slightly as she kept on dabbing. The towel came away scarlet. Merrick was standing looking down at me.

'Don't take it so hard, honey,' he said gently to the girl. 'It's only superficial.'

'Good of you to be so solicitous,' I said.

He shook his head.

'I'm not thinking about you, Mr Faraday. I'm thinking of the reaction of the bank teller when he sees your face tomorrow. Things have got to be as normal as possible.'

He reached in his pocket and came up with a lighter; he bent and lit another cigarette for me. I feathered out blue smoke at the ceiling and felt better. The girl finished fussing around with my face and stepped back.

'I think that will do, Mr Faraday. The bleeding's stopped, anyway.'

'I'm obliged,' I said.

The girl took the stuff out. The big woman was still standing by the fireplace. The whole situation seemed unreal, like we were on a stage-set waiting for something to happen. I had a lot of questions to ask but I needed to be in a little better shape to absorb the answers.

I had no guarantee of any answers, of course. But it's been my experience of characters like these — essentially amateurs despite their dangerous habits — that they don't mind talking in such situations. Especially when they intend disposing of the victim once his usefulness has expired.

I had no illusions about that. I knew a lot about the set-up at El Capitan now. They'd tipped their hand. I had only to fill in the lines between the figures, the way you make up those paintings in books. So they couldn't afford to let me go afterward. My time would run out around eleven o'clock tomorrow morning. Which gave me about twelve hours, give or take an hour or so.

Like always, I'd have to play it by ear. In the meantime there was no sense in working myself up into a lather. Merrick had gone over to the table. He came back with a package of sandwiches and a cup of coffee. He put them down on the little table by my side. The big woman's pork-pie hat was still sitting there. It looked incongruous, like everything else about this situation.

'You'd better eat this, Mr Faraday. You must be hungry by now. There's plenty more over there.'

He paused.

'But don't get up from the table.'

'I won't,' I promised him.

★   ★   ★

I tasted the coffee tentatively. It was hot and strong. Just what I needed. I finished it quickly. The girl came back into the room, her eyes searching my face questioningly. She picked up the plastic cup and silently went over to re-fill it.

The three of them sat up at the far end of the room, near the fireplace and ate and drank in silence. There was no sound except the faint crackling of the wood fire and the even fainter sigh of the wind at the windows. From time to time the big woman got up to add another log. It can get cold in the hills at night and tonight was typical.

I felt better now. I was savouring my second cup and at my request Merrick came over with a second pack of sandwiches. As I worked my way through the food I reviewed the situation. Not that there was much to review. But it was one way of passing the time.

The big woman sat at the end of the divan, silently munching. She had the Smith-Wesson down on the cushions at her side. Merrick was in another big chair the other side the fireplace, directly facing me. He had his own pistol on a small table between him and the girl. She sat on a stool the opposite side of the table, clasping her coffee cup in her two hands.

She was in profile to me and if outward

looks were anything to go by she would never have been mixed up in anything like this in a thousand years. I reviewed my chances. There weren't any. They were too far away and too heavily armed for me to try anything.

Assuming I was in any condition to do so. The Parker woman alone could have stopped me unarmed, as I'd seen. Though when I'd rested up I might meet her on equal terms if it came to fists. And providing I could move around fast enough. She'd taken me off guard up to now. It was something I would have to think about.

I looked toward the door, where a number of cases stood in the half-shadow. They'd brought sleeping bags; I could see them lying in a heap. There were travelling cases too. Things had obviously exploded up at El Capitan. Merrick was on the move.

Susan Fallowfield had taken off the raincoat she'd worn when she first came in. She still wore the tan slacks and blue shirt like she had come straight from the estate without changing, directly after our interview. I focused up on the table that stood in the middle of the room. The big oil lamp with the china base stood solidly in the centre of it. The table was a three-legged thing and wouldn't take much overturning.

The more I looked at the lamp the more I liked it. It was about the only way I would get out. If I could get to the lamp without arousing suspicion I could throw it in the fire. Or, better still, throw it at the other lamp on the mantel shelf. That would not only set the house ablaze but leave my end of the room in semi-darkness. We'd see, I was already feeling better with the coffee and sandwiches and apart from bruising and a slight limp I was almost as good as new.

The only question was when to move. It was no use waiting until morning. I had to make the play tonight. I sagged back in my chair. Merrick got up then, like he could read my thoughts. He came over and looked down intently into my face.

'The lady packs a punch,' he grunted.

'You can say that again,' I said.

He stood frowning at me like he had a

lot of things to say but had thought better of it.

'So you got Saatchi and Steevens,' he said.

They were beginning to sound like an advertising agency.

'We already went into that,' I said, 'It was them or me.'

He flinched slightly, as though I had said something that stung his sensibilities.

'You amateurs always lay it on too hard,' I said. 'You overplayed your hand.'

He shrugged.

'I don't think so, Mr Faraday,' he said easily. 'After all, we have you here and the situation is well under control.'

I sat back in the big chair and closed my eyes, like I was having difficulty concentrating.

'That depends where you're sitting,' I said.

Merrick laughed softly.

'I'd rather be where I am than where you are,' he said.

He had a point there. I knew then with absolute certainty that I would be expendable one minute after we'd come out the bank with the jewellery from the deposit box. I'd known anyway but it was nice to have it confirmed. I'd know how to conduct myself when the time came. And I knew it had to be tonight.

I needed darkness if I was to break out and get some law in. Though where I would find it up in these lonely hills was another matter. I'd think of something. I always did. I opened my eyes again and glanced at his hands as we stood there. They were empty. He'd left his pistol over on the far table. He moved between me then and the big woman at the end of the divan.

I tensed my muscles. Then Merrick had passed to the other side of me and the moment with it. I sank back in the chair. I wasn't aiming to commit suicide tonight. If I moved I wanted to have at least a fifty-fifty chance of success. There'd be time. I guessed none of them would go to bed in the normal sense. They'd be too busy watching me. I was the only free agent here. I'd find a way to play on it.

I had it then. They didn't like talking about the situation. I wanted the answers to a lot of questions. If I could needle them I might find the break I was waiting for. I felt a lot stronger now though I was careful not to show it.

Merrick reached for my coffee cup and the wrappers of the sandwiches.

'You had enough to eat?'

'Just fine,' I said.

I waited until he was halfway back across the room.

'Something's been puzzling me.'

The big man stopped, turned slowly on his heel.

'What's that, Mr Faraday?'

'What have you done with Merrick?' I said.

18

It was so quiet in the room the crackling of the fire seemed like the noise of a motor accident. I saw the girl's mouth a round O of surprise and Merrick dropped the plastic cup which went rolling and rattling over the floorboards. Only the big woman at the end of the divan sat as though turned to stone. But her slate-grey eyes were glittering now and her head turned slightly so that she could see me more clearly.

'What the hell do you mean?'

The big man in the grey suit forced the words through dry lips.

'You know what I mean well enough,' I said. 'If you're Merrick I'm Paul Newman.'

The girl was on her feet now, her features working.

'I told you he was crazy,' she said.

Only Ma Parker seemed in control of herself.

'Let him talk,' she told the peeling

wallpaper. 'I'm interested.'

'I'll bet you are,' I said.

I sat up in the chair, still trying to look exhausted, but at the same time holding their attention. I didn't want them coming close and beating me up before I had a chance to spring my surprises.

'I have the advantage of you,' I told the tall man. 'I've already seen photographs of Merrick. He's a small, fat guy with a bald head.'

The big woman laughed harshly. It rang jarringly round the dimly-lit room. The firelight made a brindled mask of her face.

'Well, well, Faraday. You do know how to get some things right.'

'I try,' I said modestly. 'And this whole set-up stank from the beginning.'

I held her eyes with my own.

'I said you were amateurs. You were making mistakes all the time. Like that dumb play in Vansittart's office when you smashed the window from the inside while trying to make it look like someone had broken in. Most of the glass was lying on the flat roof outside the window which told me immediately it was an inside job.'

The Harper woman gave me a glimpse of her unattractive teeth.

'It's all academic now, Mr Faraday.'

'Isn't it?' I said. 'But I'd still like to know the ins and outs. Just for the record.'

Merrick stood like he was a pillar of salt. The girl got up from her stool and came toward me. The once beautiful face beneath the dark Louise Brooks haircut was distorted with hatred. She looked like Bette Davis in one of her basilisk moments.

'It's all gone too far, Adam,' she told the big man. 'There's only one way out now.'

He made an imperative gesture with his left hand.

'Leave me alone, Susan,' he said harshly. 'I'm trying to think.'

The Parker woman was the only one who seemed to have kept her cool. She sat at ease near the fire, finishing off her cup of coffee, like she was still in the elegance of Vansittart's show-room.

'You'd better let me handle this,' she said.

Merrick seemed like he was coming out of a deep coma.

'We'll handle it between us,' he said thickly. 'I need a little time.'

'You haven't got time,' I said.

For a minute I thought I'd gone too far. I had sagged back in the chair like I was half-exhausted and I saw Merrick cross to the table and pick up the pistol. He brought it back and aimed it at me. Veins stood out thickly on his forehead.

'You forget my secretary has this all down on paper,' I said quickly.

That stopped him in his tracks. He lowered the pistol suddenly like he was pole-axed.

'It won't do,' Ma Parker said. 'We can take her out as well if necessary.'

'You'll have to take out the whole world before you're finished,' I said.

The corners of Merrick's lips twitched. For a minute I almost felt sorry for him, caught between the two women. But only for a moment.

'You're amateurs,' I said again. 'You were as much trapped up there on the estate as the staff. You had to cover up the real Merrick's absence and you didn't dare leave. Not until I showed up. Then it was too dangerous not to.'

I opened my eyes wide. Merrick stood holding the pistol slackly from his fingers like he was wondering where to go next. The big woman still sat at the end of the divan. The girl stood halfway between the two of them. For the first time I noticed she'd taken the Smith-Wesson from the divan next the Parker woman.

'The only real thing about the set-up was those pros you sent after me,' I said. 'Who were they? Merrick's muscle-men kept on tap at the estate?'

The tall man in the grey suit nodded.

'A man like Merrick had to have muscle on hand,' he said. 'They lived down in the lodge.'

'So you rang the gate for them to get well down the bluff and stage an accident far from the estate,' I said. 'About what I figured.'

The Fallowfield number came slightly closer; her eyes were blazing and she clutched the butt of the Smith-Wesson convulsively.

'What are we wasting time for?' she asked the big man fiercely.

'We got to take him out. We can use the girl for the bank tomorrow.'

★   ★   ★

I came out my chair like a spring uncoiling. It took them by surprise all right. It surprised me as well. My left foot kicked at the Smith-Wesson, took it right across the far corner of the room. I slammed my fist into Merrick's stomach. The pistol clattered to the floor somewhere. He cannoned back against the girl and they went down in a tangle of arms and legs.

I was up to the table now. I had the lamp before the big woman moved. I threw it as hard as I could at the chimneypiece. It exploded in a display of broken glass and blazing oil. Best of all it caught the second lamp and toppled that as well. The whole mess landed in the fireplace.

I rolled over at the violence of the explosion. Bright streamers scattered across the floor-boards in a fiery chain of white-hot flame. Someone screamed in the brilliance and the smoke. I saw the Parker woman dive sideways as the lamp landed. She was in shadow now. I kept on rolling, ignoring the muffled noises the girl and Merrick were making. I'd have a little time but the big woman was the most dangerous opponent.

If the girl had left her the Smith-Wesson the bullet would have been between my eyes by now. The room was in semidarkness except for the area of flame up round the fireplace but the divan upholstery had caught and the room was filling with acrid black smoke. I groped my way forward another couple of yards. The heat was terrific in here. I heard window-glass break then. The fire must have reached the window-drapes too.

I knew now that I'd get out all right unless I was very unlucky. It gave me extra strength. Ma Parker was trying to crawl away toward a clearer area near the room door. A fist like a ham-bone came round but I dodged away. The big woman

251

was on her feet. She came at me like a runaway rhinoceros.

She went a mile wide and I slammed one into the side of her head as she came by. She rocked and shook herself, grunting with pain. This was some woman. She turned amazingly quickly for such a massive frame. Her foot, encased in the heavy brogue, came up in a murderous arc. I caught the small table, got it between us. Even so the heavy wooden top shattered at the impact.

'No rules, Ma,' I said. 'Right?'

I slammed her in the nose while she was still unbalanced. The front of my suit was spattered with blood. It seemed like she had a geyser there. I kicked her in the stomach while she was thinking about her next move. She folded like a jack-knife. This was no time for the finer points of etiquette. I got a right to her jaw as she toppled. She was already out before her bulk started splintering the floorboards.

Susan Fallowfield came through the smoke and flame before I could turn. My shoe caught her on the knee and she stumbled in mid-stride. The Smith-Wesson blammed but the shot went somewhere up into the ceiling. Plaster rained downward. I crawled away in the smoke. She was harmless now. The house had caught nicely. I hoped some of the locals might see it. If there were any locals, that is.

I got to Merrick near the window. It was the thickest area of smoke and I put a handkerchief over my face. He was still scrabbling for the gun. I was a little over-confident by now. He'd obviously heard me coming because he wriggled aside and his boot missed my kneecap, caught me in the gut. I buckled in agony and went over the table in the centre of the floor, reducing it to tangled wood-work as I went down.

While I was holding my gut together and watching the fireworks, Merrick got to his pistol. I opened my eyes again. He was coming up through the smoke and flame like he was the Demon King in pantomime. His eyes were red-rimmed and running with the smoke. Tears ran out the corners of them but he could just about see to aim properly. The mouth of the cannon seemed to fill the entire room.

'So long, Faraday,' he said.

The window smashed then and the boom of the explosions went echoing on long after their thunder had ceased. Merrick had a stupid expression on his face as the bullets slammed him away. Four holes filled with blood were printed on his immaculate grey suit as he whirled back into the flames. I closed my eyes, smelling charred flesh.

When I opened them again the room was full of men with square jaws, wearing blue uniforms. Stella's face materialised out the smoke. She looked like one of the Angels of Mons. That is if you can believe those stories about World War One. I coughed, tears running out my eyes too.

'What are you doing in hell?' I said.

Even in that place Stella could smile. She started helping me back from the edge of the flames. Some of the police had blankets and buckets of water going now. God knows where they got the stuff.

'I couldn't let you stake yourself out

'So what was i
said.

She smiled at
sunshine that w
slatted blinds. She
of the day and
shards of sunligh
surface of the coff

'A good quest
'Though it's taken
all together. Ma Pai
crack. The police g
from the girl.'

Stella nodded, he
face, the sunlight m
her hair.

'I've been talking
the way through this ca
say it for the fifteenth
as Karen Kent knew h
force behind the whole s
widow who had a crin

like that,' Stella said. 'I sa
down the street and kept
that big woman bring y
followed. When we got h
back and found a pay phor
'Good thing you did, ho
Stella's cheek was cool
mine. I was on my feet no
over toward the far co
smoke was less dense. S
was up, holding an emp
limply in her hand. I we
it from her. Two of the
the big woman over. Sh
Susan Fallowfield look
to Ma Parker and then
a cry of anguish.

She cradled the big
'Mother!' she said
I looked at Stella.
'Even the mysteri
this case,' I said.

A big police capt
face topped with a
hair came over.
'Good to see y
Faraday. Looks lik

t in my car
watch. I saw
ou out, so I
ere I doubled
he.'
ney,' I said.
and soft against
ow and we went
rner where the
usan Fallowfield
ty Smith-Wesson
nt over and took
cops were turning
he moaned feebly.
ed wildly from me
rushed across with

woman's head.
softly.

es have mysteries in

ain with a hard, red
laming mass of sandy

ou in one piece, Mr
e we'll have to sort all

under the persona of a
pinster. There was only one
ed about and that was her

owfield was her real name?'

bout the only true fact in
ness,' I said. 'She kept her
e. The mother had an
ith Vansittart's outfit but
tious for money. She
here but she schemed for
ugh her daughter.'
te, feathering out blue
cracks in the ceiling.
educated the girl well.
came when Susan
he real Merrick on a
was a much-married
l man, far from pre-
illionaire, which was
other needed. By the
s over she was his

h-stalk over toward
y on my desk. It
Stella picked it up

fastidiously and put it in the tray with sensitive fingers.

'But Merrick was no fool,' I said. 'Despite his public philanthropy he was mean and cost-conscious. He paid the girl a small salary and she handled all the rough edges of his personal operations up at the estate.'

Stella looked at me with very blue eyes.

'The girl was his mistress, of course?'

'Of course,' I said. 'But even that didn't change things. Susan Fallowfield wanted to marry Merrick, naturally, so she and her mother could live high on the hog for the rest of their lives. Merrick didn't want that. He'd been married too many times before. But Fallowfield and her mother were tired of the status quo.'

'Merrick had never met the mother?' Stella asked innocently.

I grinned, shaking my head.

'Hardly. That would be enough to put even a man like Merrick off for life. Merrick was so mean he even hung on to his ex-wives' jewellery.'

'Which gave them a plan,' Stella said.

'Exactly. Like I said, it was amateur

stuff and it blew up more or less the first time they tried it. They had one thing going for them and that was that Susan Fallowfield had carte blanche to run the estate and the people there. Subject to Merrick's supervision, of course.'

I tipped the ash off my cigarette and focused my eyes up on the cracks in the ceiling. I took another sip of the coffee. I was getting hoarse with all this talking.

'My guess is the girl took a few of the smaller pieces of jewellery and got rid of them through her mother in L.A. But Merrick was so grasping and knew the collection so well he became suspicious. Things came to a head when the girl turned her attention away from Merrick. She couldn't get anywhere with him and she knew he would never marry her. So she formed a liason with Adam Trent, the estate manager.'

'The big man with the teeth and the grey check suit,' Stella said.

'You got it,' I said. 'When they were off the estate the girl introduced Trent to her mother, probably without explaining who she was; and they cooked up a crazy plan involving Merrick's valuables and Ma Parker at the Vansittart end.'

I looked at Stella thoughtfully.

'The police think Trent forged one or two documents relating to Merrick's property. The accountant became suspicious, but he couldn't get hold of Merrick the last few days. That's why he came up there the afternoon I arrived.'

'Thus panicking Trent and the girl,' Stella said.

I nodded.

'We'll get back to that in a minute. Like the gateman told me Merrick was becoming hard to get hold of. The girl was establishing that situation in case he had to disappear. Everything blew up when they lifted the diamond jewellery belonging to the third Mrs Merrick. From what the police have been able to piece together he went storming about the place suspecting the servants.'

Stella's eyes were very bright now.

'Merrick had shot those illegal eagles so the girl or Trent shoved the stolen property into the crop of the biggest bird.'

'Knowing it would go straight to

Vansittart's where Ma Parker would retrieve it,' I said. 'But there was a quarrel over the missing stuff and Merrick was killed, apparently by accident. Trent hit him and he struck his head on the edge of a table.'

Stella shook back a strand of blonde hair from her eyes.

'So they buried him at night on the estate, so no-one would find out,' she said softly.

'That's about it,' I said. 'The fake Merrick went on forging signatures and the girl gave orders to the estate staff like the real Merrick was still in control. But they were sitting on a keg of dynamite.'

Stella lifted her cup and drained it.

'The first thing that happened was due to the fact that those birds had been illegally shot.'

'Exactly', I said. 'So they didn't go to Vansittart's at all, but direct to Cramp's. Ma Parker didn't know where and she couldn't go around asking.'

Stella nodded slowly.

'A bit of a dilemma.'

I pushed over my empty cup.

'You could say that,' I agreed. 'There's one thing in her favour. She was rather fond of Karen King. So she concentrated her inquiries on Vansittart. She needed to get at his private files. She'd guessed, of course, that the deal was an under-cover one. But I'd been called in by then. No doubt she sized me up when I called on Karen King. In desperation she decided to go out there and try to get hold of Vansittart's keys.'

Stella got up to get me another cup. I waited until she'd come back and put it down on the blotter in front of me.

'Unfortunately for him he was in the bath and rather vulnerable. She went in through the open front door and rummaged around in his clothing. She couldn't find the keys. He came out and caught her so she had to silence him. He was running away when she dropped him with a karate chop and broke his neck.'

Stella's eyes were very bright now.

'So where were the keys, Mike?'

I grinned.

'I couldn't find them either. Vansittart had simply given them to Taki, his

Japanese gardener. They were all on a ring together with the keys that opened the garden sheds. The police found the whole bunch dangling from the lock on the outhouse where Taki had left them after quitting for the night.'

Stella smiled too.

'It wasn't their day, Mike.'

'It wasn't their case,' I said. 'The Parker woman next went back to Vansittart's and clumsily tried to break open the filing cabinets to get that address. The situation was complicated by the fact that Giles Vansittart dealt with about six outside firms. Only one of them, of course, that of Cramp, dealt with the illegal work on the protected birds.'

'Which was another reason she couldn't go around asking for them.' Stella said.

I feathered out a stream of blue smoke.

'It was a great little case,' I said softly.

'I spoiled it all by turning up at the estate. They were already off balance and they blew it by bringing in the pros Merrick had stationed up there. It's my bet he had a number of shady deals going for himself. But many men with that sort of money need to hire muscle.'

'It was all very simple, really,' Stella said brightly.

I looked at her sharply but I couldn't see any irony on her face.

'As it is, Ma Parker and her daughter will be going up for a long time and, like always, I get beat-up and landed with the slimmest of fees.'

I studied my bruises in the telephone mirror. I figured I'd live.

Stella shrugged.

'That's life, Mike.'

'It's my life,' I said. 'If you hadn't come up with those clippings I should never have known I was dealing with the wrong Merrick.'

I looked at my watch. It was crawling on toward twelve o'clock and it seemed like it was going to drag until lunch. Stella got up and took the cups back to the alcove. She returned and sat swinging a very elegant leg on the edge of my desk.

'Who gets the jewellery now?' she said.

'That's for Merrick's estate to settle,' I said.

'There's always a silver lining, Mike,'

Stella said. 'You forget we're going out to dinner with Karen King tonight to celebrate her taking over the business.'

I shrugged.

'You're right, honey. I'd maybe even stake Abel Cramp to a dinner, the way this came out.'

'No need, young man,' said a waspish voice I recognised at once.

'The whole thing's on me. I asked Miss King not to call anyone.'

Stella's face expressed surprise. I swivelled my chair. Abel Cramp was standing in the half-open door leading to the waiting room. He had on an elegant-looking suit and he was better groomed than I last remembered him.

'Do you always listen at key-holes?' I said.

He smirked and advanced into the office unctiously.

'Only when it's to my benefit, Mr Faraday.'

He looked approvingly from me to Stella.

'I'm extremely pleased with your work on this case.'

Stella smiled and ushered him to the client's chair.

'What's that supposed to mean?' I said.

Abel Cramp showed me an expanse of very yellow teeth. With his awkward build and the dusty-white hair plastered to his skull he looked more like a badly-built puppet than ever. But he was well-scrubbed and barbered and he had a bright, shining aspect about him I hadn't seen before. I could even forget his clicking teeth.

He collapsed into the client's chair while Stella went to stand behind him like a second in a boxing ring, ready with a sponge if needed. Cramp beamed across to me.

'I'm very pleased indeed, Mr Faraday. And this is to express my appreciation to you both.'

He handed me a used envelope; his name and address had been erased with a felt-nib pen and my own scribbled in its place. It was sealed with sellotape and I had a job to open it. I looked at the cheque inside. That wasn't secondhand, at any rate. I almost whistled at the amount, but thought better of it. Cramp chuckled at my expression.

'The last thing you thought, eh?' he said, slapping his emaciated thigh.

'You sure this is good?' I said.

That didn't ruffle the old boy's humour.

'Even you can't spoil my day, Mr Faraday,' he said rustily. 'I had a long talk with Miss King yesterday. Now that she's taken over the business things are looking up. She's had a chat with Van Horn. I've got the Museum of Ornithology contract.'

I caught Stella's amused eyes over his shoulder.

'Congratulations,' I said.

'And that's not all, Mr Faraday,' he said mischievously. 'There's a lady who works at Miss King's office in a secretarial capacity. A lady of mature years, you understand. She's agreed to partner me at the dinner tonight.'

'Not Ma Parker?' I said. 'I didn't know she was out on bail.'

Stella choked suddenly and the waspish expression was back on old man Cramp's face.

'Certainly not, Mr Faraday,' he snapped. 'She's a delightful lady indeed.'

'It must be spring,' Stella murmured. 'This will make five of us. That will cost you a lot of money, Mr Cramp.'

The old man chuckled, looking from Stella back to me.

'What's money, Mr Faraday?' he said slyly, like he'd made a big joke.

I put the cheque in my pocket, looking at Stella's bright face beneath the bell of blonde hair. There was a faint pinkness on her cheeks now.

'There are some things money can't buy, Mr Cramp,' I said.

PRINT-OUT
NIGHT FROST
THE LONELY PLACE
CRACK IN THE SIDEWALK
IMPACT
THE DARK MIRROR
NO LETTERS FROM THE GRAVE
THE MARBLE ORCHARD
A VOICE FROM THE DEAD
A QUIET ROOM IN HELL
HEAVY IRON
DEATH SQUAD
TURN DOWN AN EMPTY GLASS
THE CALIGARI COMPLEX
YOU ONLY DIE ONCE
HOUSE-DICK
SCRATCH ON THE DARK
NO FLOWERS FOR THE GENERAL
THE BIG CHILL
MURDER ONE
THE BIG RIP-OFF
FLIP-SIDE
THE LONG REST
HANG LOOSE
BLOOD ON THE MOON
DARK ENTRY

We do hope that you have enjoyed reading this large print book.

Did you know that all of our titles are available for purchase?

We publish a wide range of high quality large print books including:
**Romances, Mysteries, Classics General Fiction
Non Fiction and Westerns**

Special interest titles available in large print are:
**The Little Oxford Dictionary
Music Book, Song Book
Hymn Book, Service Book**

Also available from us courtesy of Oxford University Press:
**Young Readers' Dictionary
(large print edition)
Young Readers' Thesaurus
(large print edition)**

For further information or a free brochure, please contact us at:
**Ulverscroft Large Print Books Ltd.,
The Green, Bradgate Road, Anstey,
Leicester, LE7 7FU, England.
Tel:** (00 44) **0116 236 4325**
Fax: (00 44) **0116 234 0205**